praise for *Glass Animals*

Stephen V. Ramey's *Glass Animals* offers an intimate look at a matador's passion and pain, a bus driver's brush with mortality, a jilted lover's dilemma, a disfigured boy who "inhales" his salvation, and a young man hounded by glass animals in a pool. Ramey takes on the richness of his characters' emotional and physical torment and delivers something morbidly fascinating and keen. A great first collection!

Kristine Ong Muslim, author of *We Bury the Landscape* and *Grim Series*

Stephen V. Ramey captivates and mesmerizes his readers, taking us by the hand into the hidden worlds of people not unknown to us. His instincts are visceral, perceived, radiating a power and compassion that guides us inside each of his characters. Ramey's collection explores the human condition. Ramey is the real thing. Read him!

Meg Tuite, author of *Domestic Apparition*

"Gravity was another rule on another sign he could not read," Malcolm, the protagonist in the title story from Steve Ramey's wonderful collection *Glass Animals* thinks. In this gravity−defying display of mostly flash pieces, Ramey leaps and dances over the domestic and the surreal, the mundane and the magical. He seamlessly weaves a crazy−quilt of characters who – despite being a little lost and befuddled by the world – have moments of chandelier insight into their own human hearts. Reminiscent of Raymond Carver's *Little Things* and Kim Chinquee's *Oh Baby*, *Glass Animals* is a work of sparkling vision and compressed and surprising language – all put to work to reveal a world where everything's at stake.

Lori Jakiela, author of *Miss New York Has Everything* and *Spot the Terrorist*

Stephen V. Ramey lives in beautiful New Castle, Pennsylvania, a city that once rivalled Pittsburgh in industry. His formal training was in Chemical Engineering (Carnegie Mellon University), but he soon learned that his heart was not in it, and went on to work in a hardware store, a bookstore, and at a non-profit. It was when he attended a creative writing course at Indiana University that his mind opened to the potentials of literary fiction. His first assignment (*The Mailwoman*) was singled out by the instructor, Mary Austin Speaker, and there was no looking back. A flash fiction course offered by Jennifer Lynn Dawson resulted in two publications, and his membership in *Show Me Your Lits* (*http://www.showmeyourlits.com*) has resulted in many more. It's apparently never too late to learn something new.

Stephen's first novel, penned with his wife Susan Urbanek Linville, is currently making the rounds at New York publishing houses. He is the editor for the *Triangulation* anthology series from *Parsec Ink*, as well as the twitterzine *trapeze*.

He blogs at *http://www.stephenvramey.com/*

Glass Animals

Glass Animals

Stephen V. Ramey

a Pure Slush book

Glass Animals first published by Pure Slush, January 2013.
Second edition published August 2014.

All stories are copyright of Stephen V. Ramey

Front cover photograph and author photograph copyright of Susan Urbanek Linville

Cover design by Matt Potter

ISBN: 978−1−925101−86−7

You can find *Pure Slush* at http://pureslush.webs.com

Copies of all *Pure Slush* publications can be bought at http://pureslush.webs.com/store.htm

For my mother, Sharlene Reagan,
who supported me through thin
and thinner,
no matter what.
Love is like that.

and

my multi—talented wife, Susan.
I would not be
without you.

and Matt Potter,
for everything you have done
to support the craft,
and for seeing potential
in a beat down clown.

R e v e a l

Distort

Thanks

Foreword

Steve, an affable, soft–spoken fellow, came into our writers group in New Castle, PA about three years ago. It was a lightning strike. Steve is a writer's writer. He's down in the trenches with us, courageously determined to be the best story teller he can be, with the fire in the belly that drives him to do anything to hone his craft. This includes helping other writers. He shares everything, nothing left behind, willingly exposing flaws in his own work. Once he admitted that he had had to stare at a blank monitor for at least five minutes, but he got over that by typing. Another time, he submitted a story for me, because I wouldn't know a website from an armpit.

Steve's style is not a style, but a way of putting YOU in the story. "Show, don't tell" has no better advocate than his work. These stories collectively reveal a celebration of writing in as many flavors as there are jelly beans. We meet vulgarity head on, and we discover gentleness in unexpected places. Each story has its own style to fit its experience. It's that experience/style thing that makes the variety worth commenting on.

These stories are all so different, one begins to marvel at how much life experience he has had, how he sees things, and writes them so well. But in the reader's mind, the author is some person "out there" writing the stories.

I think this collection is actually a novel in which the unknown author goes slowly and irretrievably insane. Each section he gets farther from the innocent boy, and the realistic but nutty Cee Cee, and begins to see through the glass darkly. With *Refract*, a hint of the demon gets across, and *Reveal* is full of acted out fantasies and supposedly embarrassing moments which he might just be making up on the page. By *Distort*, right away we know something's really wrong, although there are glints of strange sanity in 'Cheshire Cheese' and even the talking tree in 'The Thing About Domination' (both on my fave list). By the time we get to 'Leaving the Garden', titles have gotten so far removed from stories which are so off the roof that the little boy is totally gone, and in his place is a mad vegetable bomber, wondering what will happen when / if he drops The Big One. Have we gone crazy with him? Maybe we should all be blown to bits by a nuclear cucumber.

Because, in the end, laughter is still the best medicine. I feel this in my bones. Yet I must be suspect, for no doubt I am preoccupied with mental aberrations. I just never saw someone go in quite this way. *Reflect, Refract, Reveal, Distort.* The work is both serious and absurd, a lot like life.

Perhaps this book should come with a warning.

WARNING: *This product is not recommended for treating insomnia. Side effects include feeling the headboard of your bed sliding slowly to the center of the room, giddiness, and indecision: read again or read on to the next slice of life so magically presented to you by Stephen Ramey.*

Mary Martitia Rucker, DMA
December 2012

Reflect

Into the Woods

Billy stood in the scrubland, shivering from the cold. He carried a backpack loaded with his favorite things, Teddy the Wonderbear, a book: *Oh the Places You'll Go* by Dr. Seuss – Billy wished Tiger hadn't shredded the cover, but he still liked the story fine – a peanut butter and tomato sandwich with the crust cut off. Ahead, tire tracks led into a forest of tangled trees. Beyond that, the sun was beginning to set.

Daddy had driven his Jeep into the woods two days earlier. He hadn't come back. Since Mom refused to talk about it, Billy had decided to find out for himself where the road led and why Daddy had gotten lost. It certainly did look like the sort of forest a person would get lost in. Billy found himself wishing he had saved pieces of crust to drop. That hadn't worked too well for Hansel, but was better than nothing.

A crow cawed. Others answered until raucous laughter poured over the darkening ground. Billy's gaze went to a tree taller than the others, its branch loaded with birds. The backpack dragged at his shoulder. He set it down, and knelt to pray.

"Thank you for the food we eat. Thank you for the world so sweet. Thank you for the birds that sing. Thank you God for everything. Amen." He crossed himself and started to stand, but thought better. "Please let me find Daddy," he whispered. Tears stung his eyes. "And don't let those birds get me."

Billy started walking. It seemed to take forever to cross the sandy soil. A crow launched and fell toward him. "Caw! Caw!" were the sounds in his ear, "Go away!" the words he heard.

"I'm going to find my Dad!" he shouted. The bird flapped past his head, and flew back to the tree. A shiver shook Billy so hard it nearly dislodged the backpack. He clung tightly to the strap.

He couldn't see more than a few steps into the woods. He thought of the Mickey Mouse nightlight plugged by his bed. There was another in the hall in case he had to go to the bathroom. Daddy had told him he was big enough to do that on his own. He didn't feel big enough now. He wanted to run back to the house and jump into Mom's fleshy arms. He wanted to hear her voice. He couldn't do that. He had to rescue his dad. Daddy would never leave them alone. Something had happened. He sniffed. The forest smelled of vegetation, a hint of pine sap. No trace of Daddy's Old Spice, or the Jeep's acrid exhaust.

Biting his lip, Billy stepped into darkness. A chill settled over him, dense like a blanket, only cold. He stepped again. If he stayed between tire ruts he should be all right, but what if crows were not the only thing inhabiting these woods? He unzipped the backpack with trembling fingers, and took out his sandwich. It was a sloppy mess, the bread soggy. He tore at an edge. No. Scattering bread wouldn't work; the crows would eat it.

What about tomato? Some of the chill left him. He tore apart a tomato slice and dropped a piece at his feet. His fingers slimed with peanut butter. He licked them clean, relishing the sweet smell of Mom's pantry. The feeling that went through him was like opening his eyes to the nightlight after a bad dream. Emboldened, he took another step, dropped another tomato bit.

Sometime later, he held the final sliver on his palm. "Well, I can't give up now," he said. Hearing his own voice scared him a little. He fought down his fear. "I'm going to find my dad no matter what."

"Who?" an owl hooted. Eyes glistened.

"My dad," Billy said, puffing his chest. He dropped the tomato, and continued. It seemed like hours that he walked and, still, the woods went on. The sky dimmed, then darkened. He could barely see his feet now. At least the moon was almost full. It watched over him through the canopy of twisting branches.

The cold seeped into his toes and fingers. He stomped and flexed, but it did little good. Soon, the chill had seeped into his mind too, and even his heart shivered with every beat. In a way, it was good, though, because when something rustled beside the path, he was able to ignore it and keep walking. The only warmth inside him now came from the flame of his purpose. He *would* find Daddy, no matter what.

He barely noticed the sky brighten. All of a sudden the moon was gone, and blue filled the voids between branches. He had walked all night. He should eat breakfast. He opened the backpack, and found the sandwich gone. He must have eaten it while he walked.

Weird. It felt like he had lost something else overnight too, something important. But maybe he had gained something too. He was no longer afraid of the woods, no longer afraid of the dark. A grin overtook him. Dad would say that was part of becoming a big boy. He could hardly wait to hear it from Dad's lips. His strides lengthened.

It was midmorning when he reached the forest's end. He stepped into sunshine, the warmth of it soaking his skin. The numbing cold released. He had done it! He ripped the backpack from his shoulder, and whipped it into the underbrush. He no longer needed it, was glad to be free of its clinging weight.

The road continued as far as he could see. No jeep, no Dad, no sign of habitation. Another woods smudged the distance, another woods like the one he had crossed. It was too much. Fatigue flooded over him, knocked him to his knees.

"Daddy!" he screamed. "Daddy, where are you?" Tears ran down his cheeks. Snot sagged from his nose. He brought his palms to his face, and leaned into them.

Talons grabbed his shoulder. He shrieked. A hand pulled him around until he looked into Mom's sad eyes. Her other hand held his backpack. It carried a few dead leaves, but was otherwise intact. Billy took it. It was heavier than he remembered.

"Daddy's gone," he said.

"I know, sweetie, I know." She drew Billy to his feet. In the distance, a crow screamed, then another.

Without a word, Mom led him back along the tire track path. He clung to her skirt. She smelled of apples and cinnamon, of buns rising behind the oven door glass. But there was something more complicated too, some hidden scent Billy could not grasp.

Sky Blue Pink

"Can't you just taste the possibilities?" May said, cocking an arm above one bony hip. "I'm thinking high end restaurant; lamb chops smeared with mint jelly."

"You've quite lost your mind this time," Russell said. The hall was a mess of mortar dust and broken glass. A grand piano lay overturned at one end.

"Oh, Russell, you always say that at first." She patted his arm, and bustled into the ruin.

Russell looked up, as much to avoid what he'd already seen as to see something new. The ceiling retained some of its original majesty, sweeping panels tapered to a domed center and borders of high–relief cornice. A proud place, resolute, clinging to the essence of what it once was. That must be what drew May.

She would see potential in a board slanting from asphalt. London hadn't been much more than that, an empty lot overgrown with weeds, one upright pillar and a portion of brick wall. *Do you see it, Russell? A skating rink. There's the center. Can't you just hear the children whizzing past, round and round, laughing, the clump of skate wheels on a wooden floor?*

A crash brought Russell back to his present circumstance. May had heaved a sconce onto a pile of similar refuse.

"Here," Russell said, reaching for his pocket. "I've got a match. We'll kabob lamb over the blaze."

May's laughter swirled through the hall like birds swooping.

"Six months, Russell, give me six months and you'll never recognize the place."

A knot twisted Russell's throat. Six months, twice as long as the doctors gave her. He'd brought her to Greece to spend their last days in peaceful reflection, sunsets from the beach, the taste of olives on their tongues.

She watched him, one foot on the rubble pile like a hunter posing with her kill. Her gaze was steady, expression neutral. She waited for him to make up his mind; would it be a pile of tears or a stiff upper lip?

"One more?" she said, tentative for her, assertive from anyone else.

Russell wiped his eyes. He nodded. *One more.*

"Where do we begin?" he croaked into the echoing room.

Cee Cee

Cee Cee sells C–cells at the "C" Store. She sells more than batteries, of course, the store having been in business for more than twenty years. Twenty years of Vitamin C and Club Soda and Crackers of the Animal Variety, Cardigans and Cargo pants and clip–on ties. In season she stocks carrots and cucumbers and cauliflower fresh from local fields. In winter these bins house CDs and coloring books depicting cows and cats. Some months the store pays her rent, some months it feeds on her savings. She wobbles along like a world slightly off–axis.

Today she's cleaning. Most of the store is shelves, but one end houses glass displays. Depending on how she counts, there are three or there are twelve. If she counts full counters, three is right, if she counts individual sections, twelve is correct.

"Let's see," she says, tapping glass. "A trinity or a dozen disciples. Am I the Holy Ghost or our savior?" Panes do not answer. Shelf standards say not a peep. Even the merchandise remains silent. Cee Cee stares at her bulbous reflection, and sighs. "No miracles today. No miracles today."

She begins a new sign. Magic Marker squeaks on poster board. All her signs are handmade. This one is to mark a new aisle she's squeezed into the cluttered layout. Cellophane, she writes. *Canned ... Goods?* That won't do. *Canned Comestibles? Consumables? Corn?*

The joke suddenly wears thin. She casts the marker aside. Her entire adult life has been a joke, hasn't it? The marriage she thought was true, the child that never came, the newspaper clippings so conscientiously collected, always from some inner page, a novelty human interest slant.

Derrick has left. Okay, it's been six months. She went through the motions of throwing him out, but he never actually came back to see his clothes strewn across the lawn among the pieces of his *PlayStation*. He never saw the cigarettes arranged in such a phallic manner on his recliner, tobacco scattered like dandruff.

He left her the house, the truck, even his work tools. He's never tried to take back a single thing he bought. All he wants, apparently, is that plain–faced waitress at the delicatessen with her big hips and knobby knees. She's no supermodel, that one, and none too bright or well–to–do.

It makes Cee Cee feel as if her own appearance didn't matter, or the things she did to please him. Not her cuisine – she put on thirty pounds cooking for that man – not the crotchless panties she wore for his convenience. Nothing mattered, nothing she could do. Nothing.

Cee Cee runs a cloth across the counter. Glass smears, glass clears. Depression, her friends say, and a therapist confirmed it. "I don't know the meaning of 'depression'," she told him, flashing her Cee Cee smile. "It doesn't even begin with 'c'." She won't take the pills he prescribed, won't sign up for sessions.

A clink draws her attention to the door, the day's first customer. He's tall and thin, and his face long, eyelids drooping. She doesn't recognize him.

"You got any plastic wrap?" he says, walking straight to the counter.

Cee Cee smiles, and points to her sign.

He looks confused. "Plastic wrap." He makes a box with his hands. "You know, like for wrapping leftovers."

"That's what cellophane is," Cee Cee says.

"Ah." The man nods. "Where is it?"

Cee Cee comes around and gets it for him. She has to squeeze through the narrow aisle, and curtsey down to the bottom shelf rather than a proper stoop. She brings it back to the counter, and shakes open a plastic bag.

"You've a pretty face," the man says.

Startled, Cee Cee stops in mid−motion.

"You remind me of my wife," he says. His cheeks color. "She's … she's, uh, ample too."

Cee Cee shoves the cellophane box into the bag. A dull anger warms her. Even that is welcome in a way.

"She's also quite beautiful," the man says. "I call her my sunrise after the storm." He reaches for his back pocket, then thinks better. "You sell beer here?"

Cee Cee stares, uncertain what to make of his backhanded compliment. Is he mocking her? Apologizing for his gaffe? Making conversation?

"Beer?" he says.

"Coors," Cee Cee says. She nods toward the cooler at the back of the store.

He returns with a six pack in one hand and his wallet in the other. "What do I owe you?"

Cee Cee keys the items into the register. "Cash, check, or credit?" she says with practiced ease. He gives her a bill. "Change," she says, clicking coins onto his palm.

The man pops open a can. He pops a second, and slides it across the counter.

"You look like you could use one," he says. "Loosen up a bit, girl. This one's on me."

Cee Cee sips hesitantly. The taste is sour, but wets her dry mouth. "Thanks."

"A toast." He lifts his can to hers. "To possibility."

"Probability," she says with a wink.

He laughs. "Nah, that's boring." He extends his hand. "Frank."

"Cee Cee," she says.

He laughs again. It's a boisterous sound, full of life. "How did I not know it?" He indicates the store and its C−filled signs.

Are we ... flirting? A flush blossoms through Cee Cee. She opens her senses to the cool flow down her throat. She feels suddenly young again, sitting on a blanket in the park, Dad's finger pointing past her, nearly touching her shoulder. "A bee, Cee. See?" Oh what a laugh they shared that day.

She sets the can down. "It's grand to meet you, Frank. Too bad you're married or I'd snatch you up."

He winks. "I bet you would at that." He gathers his merchandise, and walks to the door, then pauses, hand on handle. "Hang in there, girl. You'll make a go of it, just you see."

Cee Cee nods. She's been in business twenty years, yet his words ring true. He isn't talking about just a shop.

"I will," she says.

The door opens and clinks shut. The hours sign ruffles into place. *Come back and "C" us soon!*

Saint Peter's Penis

A shriveled bit of flesh preserved in glass. A penis, complete with scrotum, circumcised, the tip bulbous, the shaft stretched straight in faux erection. I turn the sphere in my hands as if admiring the miracle from different angles. In truth, a part of me is waiting for the snow to fall. The relic too much resembles a snow globe, one of those cheesy Christmas scenes enclosed in glass. My gaze finds the shadow box on my mantel. Within it, Dickens' pet Raven, Grip, perches proudly on a branch. I do not limit myself to religious artifacts.

"How much do they want?" I set the globe onto its stand, a replication of rose thorns twined into a simple crown.

"A million—five," Paul says. "I believe I can negotiate a million—two." He's a serious man. It's easier to dupe a serious man than one with laugh lines and a biting tongue like myself.

"I'll want a certificate and full history," I say.

"Of course."

"Where was it found?"

"A dig in Capernaum. Professor Sherman at the University of Haifa oversees it." Of course. Capernaum is said to be Saint Peter's home. Where better to uncover a legitimate find? Where better to seed an illegitimate one?

"Whose idea was it to package the item in this manner?" I say. "It's difficult to believe a respected scholar would allow it."

"This is as it was found," Paul says. "The globe, not the stand, which is obviously new."

"Obviously." I shake my head. "How am I to take this seriously, Paul? That someone, perhaps a disciple himself, would amputate Saint Peter's penis and preserve it in glass … is such a thing even possible?"

"Yes," Paul says. "Glass blowing tools have been recovered from as early as 50BC in Italy, and carbon dating confirms the approximate age."

"Carbon dating," I mutter. The Shroud of Turin comes to mind. Do I want to invest in an imbroglio like that?

"For glass to remain unbroken," Paul says, "buried beneath tons of rubble, to find its way to me, to you … is this not a miracle?"

"I suppose, but is it Saint Peter's penis? That's the question that matters. It's too much to hope for, isn't it, really?"

"That's what faith is for," Paul says.

How to explain it to him? That I am only too aware of the fine line between faith and gullibility? That I must be careful lest I risk a lifetime reputation on an emotional decision? Still, he *is* right. Faith is hope beyond expectation, beyond supportable fact.

"A million—two," I say. "Not a penny more."

Paul's relief shows in a quick grin. "I'll do my best," he says. Already, he's bundling the globe into soft cloth, laying it onto a bed of packing peanuts within a box several times larger than seems necessary. He bustles it through the high doorway. My butler swings the door closed. The sure click of its latch sounds. Isn't that a miracle too, that men have come to design such an intricate device?

I sigh. The four canonical gospels recount Jesus' Last Supper prediction that Peter would deny him three times before the cockcrow. Accounts differ as to how these denials took place, but they surely did. And each time, by at least one account, a cock crowed. I look to Grip, posed upon my mantel in perpetual grace. My lips pull into a smile.

"Would you have crowed, or cawed, or whatever it is you did in life, had I denied Paul?" Peter would later recant his denials, affirming thrice that he loved Jesus, and he would become the first man to enter the empty tomb. Was it less likely that his penis might survive the centuries? Surely it is better, sometimes, to reach for meaning than to know it outright.

"A million—two is not such a high price," I tell Grip. "I can afford it."

The raven remains steadfast in its silence.

The Butcher's Son

Jataka lived in faith's golden glow, oblivious to the twin treacheries of doubt and dread. When her brother, Saaras, died of a cancer in his brain she did not grieve, but instead rejoiced that he had exchanged agony for the peace of the garden above the clouds. She went on with her life.

One day her mother came to her. "Daughter, your father has decided it is time for you to marry."

Jataka's first impulse was to shake her head like a dog after a storm, and run screaming from the house to drown herself in the irrigation ditch with its slow, muddy swirls. She was not ready for her childhood to end, to belong to a man. Who was it? The bearded net−mender whose breath smelled of fish? The middle− aged bricklayer whose skin resembled mortar? None of the men her father entertained suited her. *These are not the old times*, she thought. *A modern daughter has a say in the choice of her husband.* She opened her mouth to say these things.

The tautness of her mother's expression, the slant of those brown cheeks, the inward pull of dark eyes, stopped Jataka cold. She might be seeing a mirror in this moment, a portrait of herself in twenty years, drained of youthful exuberance, exhausted with the day−to−dayness of life, praying her daughter will understand how it is and answer, 'yes'.

Jataka stared at her lap. "Who?"

"The butcher's son," her mother said.

Jataka looked up, animated by a burst of frantic fear. The butcher's son was a blob like his father, rounded shoulders, rounded face, rounded fingers like little logs of dough. She shivered at the thought of those fingers touching her.

"Is there no one better?" she said.

"Times are difficult," her mother said. Jataka saw a flash of commiseration that at least confirmed she was not crazy for loathing the butcher's son. Father must be in dire need of money.

"I will marry him," Jataka said without inflection.

Her mother nodded. "You are a good daughter." Water glistened at the edges of her eyes. She was thinking of Saaras, the son who would have brought pride to their family. The most Jataka would bring was a bride price, and not much of one if they had decided to marry her to the butcher's son.

The marriage was a simple affair with skimpy garlands, and incense so poorly manufactured the smoke carried hints of burnt fat. It brought tears to Jataka's eyes, but her betrothed, whose name was Kapi, did not seem to notice. As they knelt to pray, the tails of their garments tied into an inescapable knot between them, Jataka found herself wishing he would find a mistress soon. It was a mean thought, but she could not help it. God had put her in this position. Surely He would forgive a small amount of rebellion. She vowed to be more tolerant for the wedding night. In truth she *was* a little curious as to what that might involve. Her mother's staid rendition of duties had left her dry.

She was to discover that it involved a great deal of grunting and watching flies buzz around the ceiling fan's swaying tassels. As Kapi pounded her ever deeper into the mattress, she recalled her brother's death, the confusion in his gaze, the glisten of saliva on his lips. It had taken three men to hold Saaras down, and the violence of it had made her look away.

And then it was over, and Kapi was rolling off her, tearing the wedding sheet from beneath her wounded body, waving it out the window. "Come to the store tomorrow!" he yelled at the top of his lungs. "Every cut will be half price!"

Jataka dragged discarded clothes across her nakedness, and thought of God's grace. The ceiling fan seemed to slow. Its light smeared in her burning eyes. She turned her face into the pillow. If only she had watched more closely, she might have witnessed Saaras' soul emerge and lift to heaven. She might have observed a path to follow when the weight of this greasy, grunting man inevitably smothered her spark.

Last Call

Gary was half-drunk before we set out for the promised land of fully nude strippers and no cover charge. He knew a place on the verge of the dry county south of the city.

"They got girls there that'll melt the paint off your whiskers," was how he put it. "Nude as the Lord launched 'em, too." We'd been drinking at Bennigans, me and Gary and Tommy and Fat Fred. It being the end of the work week, Gary's suggestion carried on a voice vote. We were soon piling into his new car. Tommy sat primly behind Gary's bucket seat while Fat Fred wedged himself behind mine.

"You okay back there?" I said.

"We gotta get you laid," Fred said. It was his standard answer after ten or twelve beers. Which was pretty much every night.

"Good luck," Tommy said. "The only way you'll get Rob laid is to kill him and plant him in the ground."

"Goddam right," Gary snorted. His eyes were glassy behind his glasses.

"Should you be driving?" I said.

"You sure as hell shouldn't," he said.

I licked my lips, sweet with residue from four Amoretto and Cokes. The car backed, and turned. We started forward. Liquid sloshed in my stomach. I felt warm.

"How far is it?" Fred said.

"Twenty miles," Gary said.

"We should stop for refreshments," Tommy said. I glimpsed his eye–whites in the rearview.

Fred pointed. "7–11."

"Goddam," Gary said. "It's just down the damn road."

"Stop," Fred said. "Stop. Stop. Stop." He pounded the back of my seat.

Gary glanced over his shoulder. "You break that, you're paying for it." He pulled into the 7–11 lot. "Goddam drunk." We crackled to a stop. Tommy hopped out. I watched him browse the candy bar aisle on his way to the back of the store.

The storefront glass reflected Gary's car. Inside it, my slack face, thick glasses, overlong nose, tiny mouth. An urge came over me to throw the door open and sprawl onto the ground. I pressed my eyes tight, clamped my lips. The urge intensified. My tongue bulged as if inflating.

Then Tommy was back. Can tops gushed in rapid sequence, a pod of whales surfacing. The door chunked closed.

A cold can bumped my arm. I took the beer. When I looked over, Gary had one too. Fred belched quietly. Another can shushed. I drank mine in slow gulps, barely tasting it.

Gary resumed driving. Headlights stained the asphalt. Shadows sped by either side, punctuated by lights. Carsickness was usually a problem for me. Tonight, I felt adrift, disconnected from my senses.

Someone took the can from my fingers and replaced it with a new one. I drank automatically.

The drive stretched on. I didn't want it to end. I didn't want to return. Here I was ... what was I? Engineer? What did that mean? Blueprints, schematics, process diagrams ... did those things define me? Or did this moment between moments, when my thoughts were silver dolphins flashing? Could I capture them? Should I try?

The car lurched. I felt my head tilt. Glass against my temple, cold and pure. I did not look.

Car doors squeeched and slammed.

"Are you coming?" Gary's face hovered in bright light. I saw his angelic nature.

"No," I managed.

"Have it your way. Don't even think about hurling in my car. You feel it coming on, you open that door and lean out. Got it?"

I nodded.

"We'll be inside," Gary said.

"You have maybe two hours until last call," Tommy said. He was behind Gary now, like in one of those dioramas I'd made in Middle School. "*Comprende?*"

"*Si, amigo,*" I said. A laugh came up my throat. Gary looked uneasy, but let Tommy pry him away. The three of them glided to a cinderblock building, opened a battered green door, and stepped inside. Music throbbed and diminished.

Above me, a Neon sign depicted a woman with pointed breasts. As I watched, her position shifted, flash—flash—flash, leaning out from, then into the vertical red support post. Fat Fred's words rattled around my head: *We gotta get you laid.* A drunken giggle sloshed from my too—small mouth.

"Buy you a drink?" I said. I wondered what it would feel like to make love to a woman. I wondered what it would feel like to love myself.

Outside the car, the woman continued to move, flash after flash of blue and green and yellow, separated by instants of dark.

Blemished

There is no blemish on Carla's cheek, no purple hand–print, no red smear, not even a mottled bruise to mar her otherwise perfect skin. Still, she cannot stop herself. She looks twice into every reflection she passes, as if the first look has suppressed its reflective nature in order to shield her from herself. Out of empathy, she supposes.

In the morning, she moisturizes her cheeks, applies a concealer, then one blush dusting after another until her husband bangs the door. It never fully works, but at least it lets her feel as if she has done her best.

This morning, Karl's knock comes early. "Carla, I'm going to be late. I have to stop at the Post Office."

"Just a moment." Carla dips the brush, scrapes, applies. The next stroke is to the opposite cheek to even her out.

"I'm serious, Carla. I have a big day ahead."

"Just a moment," Carla says. She turns her face. A reddish blotch glares. *More concealer*, she thinks, but that means stripping her skin bare and starting again.

"Carla!" The doorknob rattles.

Air leaks out of her. She unlocks the door.

"It's about time," Karl mutters as he slips past.

At breakfast, Carla eats with one palm pressed to her cheek, delicately placing her fork down to grasp her coffee mug.

Karl looks up from his paper. Carla can't take her eyes from his distorted index finger. Shrapnel from an IED nearly tore that finger off in the process of killing his friend. He still wakes at night, sweat dripping, a scream frozen in his throat.

"Why can't you eat like a normal human being?" Karl says.

"Okay." She pulls her hand away a millimeter at a time.

"There," he says. "That wasn't so hard, was it?"

"No," she lies. She feels exposed. She meets his hard eyes. Usually she looks away, but today she does not.

There's a melting between them, a softening. An image comes into her: muffled silence, the muddy, bloody body of a best friend twisted at her feet, a bubble pushing up from her stomach through her chest, emerging as a scream, the scream morphing into consuming light, a flame of agony up and down her skin, toes curling inside her boots, fists clenching into balls. Then it's gone, replaced by her vanilla life.

Karl sets his coffee down. The mangled finger is red with ceramic heat.

"You'll be late," Carla says into her lap.

Paper rustles. The chair scuts. She feels Karl walk around the table, and glances up long enough to receive his morning kiss. Then he is gone and Carla's palm returns to her cheek.

Formidable Joy

Fever is a woman coaxing him to climax, tugging insistently at self, pulling it out of him. He seems to hover above the sweat—glazed carcass in the hospital bed. Chrome is his vision, the wheezing thump his new heart.

I am alive, he thinks. *Free.* And then he sees the IV bag, the descending tube. That is him drip—dripping, the clarity of his soul falling to that arm, one drop at a time. He is not free, but tethered to that body, bound to that bandage. Gravity pulls him back.

Voices. "Pablo? Pablo, can you hear me?" "Oh, Pablo, please try." "I love you, Pablo. Come back to us."

Who is Pablo? And then he is running with the bulls again. He never remembers until he is running, and then he recalls with perfect clarity. The musky smell, the press of muscle and bone from all sides, the panicked surge of adrenalin goading him to run faster, ever faster. It is a formidable joy, a sense of stampede and drifting all at once. He is content.

The stadium stands ahead, mouth open to receive him and his fellows into its vast ring. There will be peace there, an end to exhilaration. He feels bricks beneath his feet, the friction of them, the gaps in their surface. He becomes conscious of the breath tearing in and out of his lungs, the heart pounding at his chest. "Pablo!" someone shouts, and he is slowing, slowing …

§

He walks hand—in—hand with Natalia. The street is clogged with people following the eight dancing Giants and their big—headed heralds. Everywhere there is red. Red capes, red lips, red scarves. Offset by the white of other garments, the off—white of the buildings' facades. He wonders if God looks down upon this celebration and sees an artery filled with blood, red corpuscles and white cells surging to the heartbeat of this music.

The running of the bulls will be tomorrow. Is he truly ready? Has he made peace with the life he leaves behind? Switching jobs, marrying Natalia, kissing her son's head as if he had some part in the boy's life. These are barricades too.

Natalia squeezes his hand. "I wish you would reconsider. It is dangerous to run with the bulls. They do not differentiate between good and bad men when choosing whom to gore."

"Of course they do," Pablo says. "That is the entire purpose. Why do you think I run, if not to prove my worthiness to you?"

"No need for that," Natalia said. "You are worthy in my eyes."

"But do I deserve it?" Pablo waves to a Big Head, a pirate with tricorn hat, curling mustache and curled wig, all carved in painted wood. That is how he has been feeling, like a statue going through the motions of life, waving and waving and laughing inside his hollow head so that his thoughts will not be fully heard.

"You are brave," Natalia says. She kisses his cheek. "A good example for my Ramone."

Pablo waves the comment aside. Her son is a bookish boy, pale—skinned and pouty. Still, he loves Natalia, so he must also love Ramone. This is the future he has chosen.

He hopes the bull run will cauterize him from his wild past, the impulses that drove him to Natalia in the first place. She was married, but so sexy, so forbidden. Other women he had consorted with were able to drink him under the table, but Natalia was the drink itself.

Why did he stumble? He doesn't know. The bulls are almost on him when he finds his feet. Fear courses through his veins. He dodges for the side barricade, but it is already too late. Pain, as the horn gores his buttock, an agony as if someone has stuck a red hot poker up his ass. He cries out. A second pain, this one less intense.

Black.

Grey.

Storm clouds above. The day is cool, if humid.

"Do you want to go back?" A woman's voice, deep and scratchy. Heavy smoker, perhaps. She stands on an endless shore. Long grey waves lick the beach. Hiss, slide. The breath of the world. He listens for its heartbeat, but hears his own instead.

"Who are you?" he says.

"Do you want to go back?" she says.

"Of course I do." The bull run flashes, intense, alive. He feels the horn again, again, again, the pain like a new pulse.

In both hands, the woman lifts a curved horn to the sky. It crumbles to ash, and drifts down.

§

Ramone looks up from his birthday cake, eyes resentful. With full might, he blows out candles.

Pablo feigns a smile. Ramone's wish hangs between them. *I wish you dead, Pablo.* Natalia's smile shines in the dim room. She does not see this subtext.

"I am the way," the woman says. Pablo's eyes fix on the ash at her feet. Waves slide closer with each cycle. Her meaning is clear. He must eat of the ash before the tide claims it if he wishes to return to his life. He walks to the woman, and kneels. He reaches down, uncertain.

"The church has granted the annulment," Natalia says. "Once it is final, we can be married."

They lie in bed, sheets wet with their sweat, and wrinkled around them. Pablo wonders what God sees. *Passion? A pastry?*

Natalia's fingers play down his ribcage. His skin leaps at her touch as it always does.

"Do you love me?" She nibbles his mouth, his neck, his chest.

He feels passion rising, a fever throughout his body begging to be stoked. Stirred. Released. He stares at the mirrored ceiling as Natalia's hand folds around him.

A wave hisses close, a voice he cannot understand.

The Divide

"… as if you're on the other side of a divide," Dad said as he stomped down to breakfast the morning of his fifteenth anniversary. Not quite fifteen myself, I sat at the table, an old pine oval with legs that angled down to the floor with shaky purpose.

Mom was already making eggs, scrambled for me and her, poached for Dad. She wore the apron he had bought her for their fourteenth anniversary. *Kiss the Cook*, it said above full, red lips that reminded me of Mick Jagger (of all things). I tugged at a bra strap and thought of the rash developing under my right breast.

Dad sat in his chair, and unfolded his paper. He seemed to have forgotten whatever he was talking about. It was not unlike him to blurt random thoughts. That drove Mom crazy sometimes, but usually only made me curious. How can a mind work like that, so passionate and dispassionate by turns?

When we finished eating, Dad said, "Sometimes I feel like I'm talking across a canyon."

"Then don't talk," Mom said. Dad raised the paper.

"I feel it too," I said, and waved vaguely above the cluttered table. I could picture it in my mind, a canyon, boulders like bits of crust strewn far below my vantage, the winding river that ran through it, the echo it protected. The egg in my belly settled into mush, beginning its journey toward digestion.

"Must you encourage him?" Mom said.

I shrugged, and sprinkled pepper across my plate. A canyon was a divide, wasn't it, a lack of groundwork, a chasm unfilled by substance? It was all around me, that absence, that unknowing we ignored. I thought of Dad behind his paper, shielding me from his

49

confusion. One plus one is two. But is it always? Everywhere? Does there exist a time and place where it is not? I lifted my glass, and tilted orange juice into my mouth. The pulp on my tongue was something, little logs of sweet—sour that contrasted the feeling of the juice sluicing through.

I took my plate and glass to the sink, and set them carefully within. *Another canyon.* I ran water, watched it bunch up, then spiral down into the drainpipe.

Dad brought his plate. "What do you see?" He stared down the drain, as if he had caught my transfixation.

"You two look so cute," Mom said.

Dad waved her over. She untied the apron as she walked, and I saw the outline of the bra beneath her blouse. Her breasts were round and proud, everything mine were not. I wondered if that was something you grew into, or were born with.

"Do you realize how long it's been since we've been together like this?" Mom said.

"Twelve hours?" I said.

She shook her head. "You're usually listening to music or online with your friends, and your dad is watching the television, and I'm fumbling through a cross—stitch."

"Mom, we're looking down a drainpipe," I said.

"We're together," she said, and her warm palm was on my neck, her lips in my hair. For an instant, I felt it too. We were connected in ways the divide could never conquer.

I leaned to the sink and yelled, "Hulloo." Dad cocked his ear as if listening for the echo. His stomach gurgled.

50

Smiling, Mom shook her head. She started to clear the table. The tenderness did not leave her expression, even when Dad let loose a squishy fart.

He gave us a sheepish look. "Happy Anniversary?" he said, and the three of us broke out in laughter.

Refract

You Say *Tu Dou*, I Say *Ma Ling Shu*

"Crazy," Hmong says. "Just crazy. Millions of Renminbi floating between pockets, but I cannot find a good woman. All they want is land."

"Loveawake.com," May Chin says. She is a beautiful flower on Hmong's laptop screen. High cheeks, lovely oval eyes, thick, straight hair. She is, of course, married. And living across the Taiwan Strait in Taipei. And pregnant with her second child. Hmong sighs. When he contacts May Chin, his computer becomes a window, and she is in the next room. He must remember that he speaks to her virtual self.

"That is a Taiwan site," he says. "I have enough problems without visiting suspicious websites."

May Chin laughs. "Men seeking companionship online cannot be unexpected."

"They've probably blocked it," Hmong says. "In the States, you can see all sorts of perversity on the internet. Here, it's a buffet of only *tu dou*."

"*Tu dou?*"

"Potato," Hmong says.

"Ah, so sorry. We say *ma ling shu*."

Hmong laughs through a throat worn raw from screaming at the stock exchange. He prays it will not hurt May Chin's beautiful ears. "You have forgotten your root," he says.

"A joke," May Chin says. "The potato is a root, just as is our ancestral tree. You reveal a deep dimension, Hmong. Here in Taiwan the girls would be draped over you three thick."

"I'm not in Taiwan," Hmong says.

"That is your choice," May Chin says. Hmong's shoulders pinch. While it is true the Communists have relaxed their grip, they retain many tools of oppression. There is every possibility this discussion is being recorded.

"We're together now," he says. "Like a root from *Zhongguo,* technology connects us through a network deeper and wider than a man can know."

"It is not real," May Chin says. "You cannot eat technology as you can *ma ling shu.*"

"Anyone can grow potatoes," Hmong says. "We're growing cities. Our trees blossom millionaires, yet we have too few women, too little opportunity, too much corruption. Still, it is a hopeful time."

"China remains China," May Chin says. "The fields will demand blood at some point. It is not too late to leave, Hmong."

"I have family here," Hmong says, "and money in my pocket. That's enough." *For now.*

"Loveawake.com," May Chin says. "The first step in a voyage is to find a boat and someone to row it. Women are more than love pillows."

"Perhaps," Hmong says. "I am open to experimentation."

"You remain the scoundrel I knew as a child," May Chin says. "I must make dinner." She stands, hand going to her bulging stomach. Hmong's heart skips. There is the son or daughter he will never have unless his financial situation improves.

The Skype application closes, revealing a photo of cranes towering over Beijing. The past is in the process of collapsing, the future uncertain. He would give much for love, but not everything. His gaze drifts to the closed door. The click of his laptop closing hangs forever in his ears.

The Girl Who Turned Down Pizza

It's the strangest thing. Today was supposed to be the day. We discussed it last night in the car, her creamy ankle draped over my thigh, her face flushed from some serious kissing.

"Tomorrow?" My voice was a little flushed too, truth told. It wasn't my first time, but she was some kisser.

"Tomorrow," she confirmed. "I want to be certain. I don't want to do this impulsively."

"Sure," I said. "I can wait. You're worth it."

So here we are, strolling in the backyard by that old swing set her father built. Her parents are at work and we're skipping school. The perfect setup.

She lays out the blanket. I pull down my pants. She starts unbuttoning that sexy day dress – it's yellow, my favorite color – and hangs it from a nail. I almost fall down tugging my t–shirt over my head.

She's stepping out of her panties when the first car door slams. Her mouth goes round. She reverses course, ripping her panties back up over those taut thighs.

"No, it's okay," I say. "I guess I forgot to tell you. I invited a few friends. Jimmy and Klaus. And Simon." Simon owns the camcorder. But, it's already too late. She hobbles toward the tree line, working the dress strap over her shoulder.

"Come back," I yell. Nothing, not even a glance. So much for being patient, listening to her needs, yada yada.

Simon pushes his glasses up. "Think she'll come back?" He fits the camcorder into his hand, and aims it at me. He's bluffing. He'd never waste battery on a guy. He's gay, but not like that.

Klaus plops down. He opens a pizza box on his lap. A peppery smell wafts. He's the opposite of Simon, big and wide. "Did you tell her we were bringing food?" he says.

"Nah, I forgot."

"There's your problem," Jimmy says. He sits on a swing. A rhythmic creaking starts. "Girls don't put out for nothing."

"Should we wait for her?" Simon says.

"I don't know. She already kept me waiting an entire night." Yellow flashes in the tangle beyond the yard. Is she watching us? I remember birds scoping out Mom's feeder, a yellow warbler among all those sparrows and starlings. It was beautiful. *Sweet–sweet–sweet, I'm so sweet*

"Who can figure girls?" Jimmy says. "Show them a good time, they turn you down. When you don't want them, there they are." He hops off the swing. "I say let her fend for herself."

"Yeah, I guess." I watched for the warbler the next day and the next, but it never returned. That's the trouble with birds. They can fly anywhere while we're stuck here on the ground.

"More for us," Klaus says, lifting a pizza slice to his mouth.

Collision Course

Ralph drives a bus for the city. He used to own a taxi cab. He made better money there, but the robberies were stressful, particularly that last one. He'll show you the bullet hole if you ask, a dent in his upper arm like a pothole covered with skin.

God reminded him that day that money doesn't matter. Money is as imaginary as the square root of negative one. This mantra appears on the opening page of the notepad in his shirt pocket where he records random thoughts. Yesterday, he wrote this: *If Boston trades Youkilis for cash, is it suicide?* He was thinking of prostitution at the time, how some women trade sex for money. That's the ultimate juncture of the real and unreal to his way of thinking. Sex is real. The slapping of flesh on flesh creates a cadence that sends the mind flying. Money, on the other hand, is created by banks to keep people like Ralph perpetually in debt. Women are idiots to devalue their sexual capacity with money.

The imaginary casts real shadows, Ralph thinks. The shadow of money is debt, the shadow of security, adventure, and love's shadow? He hasn't deciphered that one. It may be despair, it may be hope. It certainly is not hate. Hate casts its own shadow.

Ralph's wife left him for a plumber. He did more than snake their shower drain, it turns out. Ralph refused to pay the bill. His wife took the house and part of his savings when a judge put their imaginary holdings into an imaginary box, and sawed it into very real halves. She included the plumber's bill as debt, thereby soaking Ralph for half of it.

Some days Ralph tells himself she deserves a windfall for standing by him in his taxi days. She deserves it for raising the kids. He imagines this is so, but his gut knows better. The plumber has money. Why couldn't she leave Ralph his own?

Ralph hates driving a bus. All that stopping and starting, impolite cars, impolite passengers, dispatch scratching at his ear. He'd quit if he could, but the economy is bad. The economy is imaginary: market cycles, busted bubbles, stock market trends. *Capitalism's shadow must be peace, or maybe war.*

No, he doesn't hate driving a bus, he loathes it, an emotion more active than hatred.

"Loathing," he mutters. He releases one hand from the giant wheel, and digs the notepad from his pocket. He writes: *Loathing is the shadow of love.* He crams the notepad into his pocket, and sets his hand back upon the wheel. It vibrates loosely beneath his palm.

A ding. Ralph looks into the rearview. A lady with shopping bags has pulled the emergency cord.

"You missed my stop," she says.

So I did. Ralph pulls over and lets her out. He flashes his blinker, and merges into traffic.

For a time he pays attention. There are eight passengers when he stops at Sampson. He picks up six and lets off four. At Main, he lets off two, and picks up one. Hermitage is deserted. He barely stops there at all. Commonwealth comes. Three get on, and five depart.

How many are on the bus now? This is a game he plays to get him through the grind. Eight plus six minus four minus two plus one is nine. Nine minus five plus three, leaves seven. Seven passengers remain. He looks into the rearview.

The bus is filled, every seat taken.

"This won't do," he says. "It isn't right." He looks again. Nearly every eye is trained on him.

61

"You shouldn't be here," he says. "Only seven, the answer is seven." He slows the bus. Horns honk behind him. A passing motorist flashes the finger out his window.

"Which of you is real?" Ralph says. He blinks hard. The bus remains filled. "Answer me," he shouts. "Only seven of you are real." He tries to recall faces, but can't. He barely looks at passengers as they get on and off. To him, the men are all plumbers, the women wives.

Grumblings sound. People stir. A few stand. More than seven. *Too many.*

Ralph stands too. He will confront them, and make the unreal disappear through observation. *Yes. No.* The lead passenger is as wide as the aisle, black as sin. He has a thug's face. *Security is an illusion too.* Ralph collapses onto his seat. The line of people moves forward. He jams his foot on the gas pedal. Momentum throws its weight. Grunts sound, bodies domino.

The bus strikes a car, another. It leaps the curb, hurtles a wrought iron fence. People in tuxes and crème−colored dresses scatter. Tables crash. *Thump−a−bump−a−thump* goes the bus. Ralph jounces in his seat.

They slam through plate glass. A billiard table skids. Faces flash, someone shouts. Ralph sprawls over the wheel. His head strikes something hard.

It's over. Debris patters through the eerie silence.

Ralph wheezes in and out. Blood mists from his mouth. *Did it work?* When the imaginary collides with reality, the two must cancel. It's simple math, or maybe Physics.

His heart stutters. He thinks of his wife with the plumber, their bed bouncing like a plunger, her eyes round and wide. His focus draws in on his dented arm, the hole that is not a hole, a bullet wound bandaged with skin. It's the only thing he knows is real.

Simply Salazar

When his girlfriend dumped him, Salazar suppressed an urge to stalk her. That would only lead to trouble, maybe even a double–murder. She said she wasn't seeing anyone, but why else? It was probably that guy down at the hardware store. Sandy hair was a definite weakness of hers. It was why he'd worn a wig for the full week of their relationship. Had she seen him take it off? He should ask. He picked up the cell phone and thumbed through to her number.

Rrrring! Rrring!

"Hello Salazar."

"Hi Claudia. I just wanted to ask you if the reason you broke up with me –" The line went quiet. He pressed redial.

Rrring! Rrring! Rrring! Rrring! Rrring! Salazar closed the phone. Maybe she was driving. He should buy a hands–free set for her car. In fact, that's what he would do.

He rode his bike down to the strip mall. He'd thought about getting a driver's license many times, but had never made it through the DMV line. The bike suited him fine anyway. It was usually sunny in San Diego.

The hardware store was near the far end of the mall, but the parking lot was laid out in such a fashion that riding a bike could be dangerous. Salazar dismounted, and walked it along the sidewalk. People bustled past, not paying him any attention.

He came to the store. There was a bike rack outside with two bikes already parked. He looked through the door, and saw Sandy–hair talking to a customer. As he spoke, his hands made expressive gestures, palms cupped and sweeping in small circles as if he were feeling Claudia's breasts. She hadn't let Salazar do that, but she would let him. He had that going for him.

"I wonder what they feel like," Salazar said. He locked his bike beside the others. It wouldn't hurt to ask.

The chromed top of a RustOleum can caught his attention. How did they get that shiny finish to stick to a plastic lid? How hard would it be to peel it off? He walked to the display, and lifted the can in one hand. It was heavier than it looked, but what wasn't? He rubbed at the chrome with his index finger. It was smooth. He scratched with his nail. Nothing. *This is one admirable lid*, he thought.

"Can I help you?" Sandy—hair stood at his shoulder. His eyes were translucent green. Salazar saw what Claudia saw in them.

"Hold this," Salazar said, pushing the can into Sandy—hair's hand. He reached into his khaki shorts pocket for his pen knife.

"You don't need that," Sandy—hair said. "Look." He squeezed the lid, and popped it free.

Ouch, Salazar thought. He opened the knife, and took the lid from Sandy—hair. He scraped the blade across its surface. Chrome flaked to the floor.

"Dude," Sandy—hair said, "you can't do that. Now you gotta buy the can."

"Have you been seeing my girlfriend?" Salazar said.

"What?"

"My girlfriend," Salazar said. "Have you been seeing her, dating her? You know what I mean."

Sandy—hair frowned. His gaze fell to the open blade. Salazar closed the pen knife, and dropped it into his pocket.

"What's her name?" Sandy–hair said.

"You tell me."

Sandy–hair blew out a breath. "Are you for real? You know you're buying this can, right?"

Salazar watched Sandy–hair's mouth. He imagined those plush lips on Claudia's. It wasn't hard.

"I'm dating a girl from the Community College," Sandy–hair said. "Her name's Marcy."

"No," Salazar said. "That's not her."

Sandy–hair nodded. "Come with me. I'll ring you out."

"Do you have any hands–free phone setups."

Sandy–hair shook his head, and walked to the register.

Salazar motioned with his hands. It felt clumsy. "For cars."

"I know what you mean," Sandy–hair said. "We don't carry those. You should try Best Buy."

"It's for my girlfriend," Salazar said.

"That's cool." Sandy–hair scanned the RustOleum can. A number came up on the digital display.

Salazar opened his wallet. It was empty. "I don't have any cash."

"Credit card? We take all the major ones."

Salazar shook his head.

"Maybe that's why you're having girl problems," Sandy–hair said. The words were mean, but the way he said it was nice. Compassionate. *Sandy hair, green eyes, compassion.*

"Tell you what." Sandy–hair set the can on a shelf below the counter. "Give me your name and phone number, and I'll hold this for you until you get some money, okay?"

"That's a great idea," Salazar said. *Intelligent too.* He certainly saw why Claudia was interested. "Can I have your number too? I'll call before I come in to make sure you're working."

"Here's a store card," Sandy–hair said.

"Can I have your cell number?" Salazar said. "I'll feel nervous if you don't answer."

Sandy–hair looked him up and down. "I guess so." They exchanged numbers.

Salazar left the store, and unlocked his bike. He walked it along the sidewalk, feeling better than he had all day. The sun warmed his head. He thought of Sandy–hair's gleaming eyes. The end of the sidewalk came up. He started to lift his leg over the seat bar, but thought better. He pushed the kickstand down and leaned the bike to rest.

He pulled the cell phone from his pocket and deleted Claudia's number. Hands–free sets were expensive anyway. Then he dialed Sandy–hair. It wouldn't hurt to ask when he would get off work tonight.

Rrring. Rrring. Rrring.

"Hello?"

Jehovah Joint

Witnesses scoured the land with their droning promises of eternal salve. From a peephole that made the world outside even smaller, Jeremiah Wilson, retired college professor and disciple of the hemp, watched a pair of them stride up the stoned walkway to his porch. He undid the security chain, and turned the knob lock. He opened the door.

"We bring the good news of the Kingdom to your doorstep, neighbor." The speaker was tall and elegant, a man with bright green eyes and thin lips. His suit was recently pressed, and seemed to faintly glitter. "Are you familiar with Jehovah's undeserved kindness and the Kingdom of hope?"

"Want a brownie?" Wilson said. He offered a plate through the doorway. An aura of sweet marijuana smoke hovered.

The speaker frowned. "The plate is empty, neighbor."

Wilson chuckled. "Did I say it wasn't?"

"You mean to tempt us with an empty plate?"

Wilson winked. "Takes one to know one." He withdrew the offer. "If you'd come a few minutes earlier it wouldn't have been empty. I guess I got tired of waiting."

The second man quoted: "If we stop actively supporting Jehovah's work, then we start following Satan. There is no middle ground."

Wilson nodded. "Can Jesus microwave a burrito so hot that he himself cannot eat it?"

"What?" the speaker said.

The quoter's brow furrowed. "The path of the righteous ones is like the bright light that is getting lighter and lighter until the day is firmly established."

Wilson flicked a burning joint onto the porch. It smoldered lazily, smoke flowing along the quoter's pant leg. The speaker licked his lower lip, a reflex action, no doubt. He had partaken of the weed. Wilson watched him watching the younger man. Would he stand firm or step back?

The quoter performed an interesting compromise, maintaining his lead foot while withdrawing the other until he looked something like a sprinter preparing to take his starting stance.

"This one is lost in Satan's grasp," he said.

Wilson shook his head. "You don't believe that or you wouldn't be here." He cleared his throat. "Let's see, now, John 16:13 as I recall: When the spirit of the truth arrives, he will guide you into truth, for he will not speak of his own impulse, but what he hears he will say, and he will declare to you the things coming."

The speaker looked thoughtful. "You have studied the page, but do you understand its meaning, Mr ...?"

"Name's Jeremiah," Wilson said. "And, yes, I have a passable understanding, though we should both admit that some meanings come from inside the head and others do not."

The speaker blinked.

Wilson stepped aside. "Come on in. Don't mind the clutter. My cleaning man is incapacitated." He indicated Frank snoring on the couch, a shock of white hair protruding from his scalp.

"We abhor clutter," the quoter said. "It is our duty to sweep clear the heads of those who would be saved."

Wilson pressed a broom into the man's hands. "Have at it. Might I suggest you begin with those cobwebs?" He pointed to a mass of dusky web that would have made the most extravagant haunted house jealous. The quoter stabbed tentatively as if expecting spiders to pour forth.

Wilson led the speaker into a kitchen layered in flour dust. Someone had been baking recently and it had not gone well. A table leaned into the wall on three legs, the surface smeared with brownish substance.

"Sit," Wilson said. He set the plate on a counter.

"There's only one chair," the speaker said.

"You are my guest," Wilson said. He lifted a bowl and wiped a finger along its brim. He extended it toward Speaker. "Batter?"

"No," the speaker said. He sat. The chair tilted precariously. "Might I offer you Jehovah's bread in place of that dark substance?"

"Sure," Wilson said. "I'm up for anything."

The speaker steepled his fingers. "For us to be acceptable to God, our sincere beliefs must be based on accurate information. I will be happy to assist you in examining what is involved in serving God with sincerity and truth."

Wilson laughed. "Didn't you people predict the Second Coming, like a thousand times?"

The speaker withdrew his arms from the table. His sleeves pulled reluctantly from a tarry substance. "Even the Apostles made mistakes," he said. "This does not excuse us trying to understand Jehovah's will, to seek his spirit and draw it close about us."

"I like that," Wilson said. "Cloak of the Christ, plus 5 versus demons."

70

"I don't understand your reference."

"Now you know how I feel when you show up at my door."

"I doubt that," the speaker said. "My reasoning is sharp. Your thoughts are muddied by the drugs you consume."

"Or maybe it's the other way around." Wilson produced a wadded joint from his pocket and pressed it carefully to his lips. The speaker's expression showed disdain. His eyes did not.

Wilson spoke carefully around the stub: "That's how it is with weed, neighbor. The fuzziness clarifies the longer you hold it in you. Soon enough it's the sharpest logic." He flicked a lighter, lit up, and inhaled the smoke deep inside.

The speaker's lips puckered subtly.

"You want a hit?" Wilson said, voice gone high in his attempt to minimize his lungs' loss.

The speaker glanced through the doorway. In the living room his companion leaped up and down, broom extended. He looked back, lips ticking into a smile that, surprisingly, did not shatter his elegant face.

He reached.

Would You Be Wiser?

Imagine. If you had been born from a milkweed pod, your hair white with old age and wrinkles on your face, would you be wiser? As the husk split, as the edges of its protection pulled back, would you devise a way to reclose it? Would you concoct a glue from spit and floating dust, make staples from pulled bicuspids? Would you sacrifice your skin to patch that breech in your cozy isolation?

Canis ex Machina

Clarise in her cowboy boots, lying on the porch with that mangy dog. That's what I remember about that day. That, and her mother screaming. *This is the last straw, you hear that, you freeloading sumbitch?* How could I not hear? The entire county must have heard. And so I left, but as I pulled away in the beat up pickup I'd bought down at the Good Year Shoppe – no, they weren't selling trucks, just tires; I talked them into throwing in the truck for an extra grand – as I pulled away, the look on Clarise's face in the rearview about tore my heart out. We were close, that girl and me. Close as feathers in a fat man's pillow.

There I go again. I got ahead of myself, which is halfway most of my problem when I think about it. I'm always reaching before I think, puckering up before I see whose lipstick I'm about to taste. It's a real issue with me, I freely admit it.

Anyway, Clarise and me. She's a chubby ten–year–old with her mom's dishwater blond hair, and big blue eyes. Smart as sin, too. I asked her once – I was helping her do some homework – what was twelve times twelve, and she looks at me without blinking, and says, "Gross." Then she giggles and punches my arm. I just kind of chuckle and move on to the next problem. Two days later, it dawns on me what she meant, and I start laughing so hard I have to pull the truck over. Tears on a grown man's cheeks in Texas, there's a sight you don't see too often.

I met Clarise's mom at the diner. She'd been working there for something like twelve years. I knew right away I had to have her, with those long legs and sassy smile. Three days later we were humping in a sleeping bag out back of her house. She didn't want to wake Clarise. It was the dog she should have worried about. There we were, on the verge of sealing the deal, and that dog starts woofing up on the second floor, paws spread on the inside of Clarise's window. *Oof! Oof–oof!*

Her mom scrambles for her bra – "Dammit, Sam, I told you not to be so loud! – but it's already too late. Clarise ducks away. The dog drops down out of sight too. Her mom charges inside.

I flop onto my back, smoke a Marlboro, and watch me some stars. I wonder sometimes if maybe there isn't a star out there just like Earth, with people like you and me, and animals and trees, only the women are naturally polygamous – that means they tolerate men a whole heck of a lot more than they do here. What would life be like on a star like that? A man can dream.

A little later, the screen door squeals and that scroungy dog comes charging out, dragging Clarise's mom behind it. "Walk the dog," she tells me. I got a whole other kind of dog walking in mind, but she won't have none of that. "Walk the damn dog!" And so I do, only I don't put on pants. If the neighbors complain about some guy in a cowboy hat wandering around scratching his balls at midnight, she's got no one to blame but her own self. And I sure did not pick up any shit. Not this Texas boy.

So, morning came around, and there's Clarise sitting at the kitchen table, stirring a spoon around a bowl of soggy cereal, and she says to me point blank. "You ain't the first to screw Momma on the lawn."

"Didn't think I was." I like to play it cool with kids. My dad was an asshole, used to beat us six ways to Tuesday. I would never beat a child. "The thing is," I said, "I like your mom a lot, and I hope that maybe, in time –"

"You like dogs?" she said. And right on cue, the mutt's head appears above the table. He must've been laying at her feet.

74

"Sure," I said. And I mostly do, too, though I can do without poodles, and those little ones with the sausage body and pointed teeth, you know, the Mexican ones.

Clarise looked over her shoulder, then to the door, then back at me. "I'm going to explain this to you one time." Her eyes got real serious. The spoon clinked against the bowl's edge and toppled to the floor. I heard the dog lapping.

"My momma can take care of herself," Clarise said, "but if you ever hurt my dog, I'll skin you like a rabbit."

"Sure," I said. "I understand."

"No, you don't," she said. "I don't mean I'll lock myself in my room and cry a blue streak. What I mean is I'll take this knife –" and she lifted a butcher's knife from the empty chair seat next to her " – and I'll skin you like a rabbit."

Something about the way she said that made me swallow twice.

"Good," she said, "then we understand each other." She put the knife back, and retrieved the shiny–as–new spoon. "Cletus is my friend. Friends look out for each other."

I nodded. "I'd like to be your friend." It came out kind of weak, but the feeling was real strong. Clarise might be ten, but she was the woman I had been looking for. Not in a sex way – that don't turn me on – but in a, I don't know, *deeper* way, I guess.

She started eating. "You want me to call you Mister Cannon, or Sam?" she said like it was the first conversation we'd had.

"Sam," I said. "Please."

And that's how it was until I screwed things up with her mom. It wasn't entirely my fault, mind you, that other waitress came on to me. She wasn't as pretty as Clarise's mom, but she had a little fire going on down there in the caboose. "What do you want on your wiener?" she says. I mean, really, right? So I ask her if she likes her buns toasted, and the rest is history.

Well, I guess that catches you up to the present, other than the two—day binge. I'm mostly sober now. Oh, and I didn't tell you about the dog leaned out the passenger window, but then you wouldn't be surprised if I did, so I won't apologize for that. I have a plan. I snatched the dog while Clarise was at school and her mom was at work, and now I'm off to the print shop to have some flyers made up. What do you think about this for wording?

Found: Large dog, off—white, answers to the name of Cletus. Call 555—1212 (you're crazy if you think I put my real number here). *Reward: One sorry—ass guy who will never do it again.*

Now, I'm not pretending Clarise's mom will pick up on that code, but I'll bet anything Clarise will figure it out. And she'll find a way to bring her mom around. That's the thing about that girl. Smart as a whip, and loyal to her friends. I may not be one of them after our little falling out, but I'm banking on Cletus.

Desperation

She figured if she stood outside the church in her wedding gown long enough someone would take the hint. She hoped he would be gainfully employed, own his own car, maybe have enough left from his paycheck to take her to the movies once a month. She hoped his mother was not a bitch. She hoped he would be good in bed, not like her ex—boyfriend. She hoped he would know his way around the barbecue too. It was a little selfish, but she did like her barbecued ribs. "Blame Daddy," she would tell him.

The Mailwoman

When the mailwoman collapsed on the doorstep, neighbors claimed they saw Frank Rowe take his mail from her fist and storm inside, angry it was mostly bills again. What he really did was check the woman's pulse, then hurry without quite running to the phone.

The ambulance came, and two burly men hurried through the chain−link gate, up spalled cement steps to the porch where they deposited boxy equipment beside the woman's face (blocking the view for Janice March next door, who was taking notes).

They proceeded to revive the woman, undoing three buttons to plunge a syringe directly into her quivering heart, placing an oxygen mask over her mouth. All this while Frank Rowe *leered*, Noreen Perkins would report from across the street. The truth is his mouth did gape, but only because he had not been so close to death since his brother's funeral last spring.

As the men bundled the mailwoman off on a stretcher − naked as a blue jay according to Jennifer Strong − he noticed their resemblance to pallbearers, and winced. A wince is *not* a smile, no matter what Francine Jenkins told her husband.

And when the lead man stumbled, the rusted gate snagging his uniform pants, Frank Rowe laughed outright a majority of the women recounted. Yet his doubling over was not the result of some reflexive cachinnation, but a physical pain in his gut, a metaphorical kick to the solar plexus resulting from a momentary vision of his brother's pallbearer tripping, the body sliding from the splintered pinewood coffin amid a confusion of flowered wreaths and wire stands. "You get what you pay for," Frank's wife had later commented, meaning the coffin.

That night at the Moose Lodge he listened to the tragic tale unwind second—hand from various husbands, to the laughter that accompanied his complicit actions therein, and he smiled. A simple smile to be sure, nothing fancy. He had never been one to stand in the way of fun.

Afterward, when they bought him a round and toasted his antics — *Stealing the mail from a convulsing mailman? Talk about post haste!* — he only pretended to drink.

Christmas in Nicaragua

Kervin runs before me, legs and arms pumping, mouth wide with joy. A half—filled sackcloth jounces from one fist. I cannot run so fast in my knee—length dress, but I try to keep up. We race to the brick house on the corner. Behind us, a stream of children flop and flap in their Sunday garb, a procession of innocence in search of the best treats.

We pull up at the porch, wrought iron railing, concrete floor. Kervin starts us: "Hail Holy Queen enthroned above, O Maria." I join in. "Hail Mother of Mercy and of love O Maria." Soon, the whole yard is singing the seasonal hymn.

> *"Triumph all ye Cherubim*
> *Sing with us ye Seraphim*
> *Heav'n and earth resound the hymn*
> *Salve Salve Salve Regina"*

And the door opens to reveal a chubby face, a boy with pug nose and wide set blue eyes. His features are American, which means his parents are rich. Christmas spirit swells inside me, a blessing of light and love.

"What is the cause of our happiness?" I scream.

"The conception of the Virgin Mary!" others shout. The singing resumes, out of tune, out of cadence. It doesn't matter.

A woman appears in the doorway, long legs swathed in blue jeans, yellow hair falling to her shoulders. Her cheeks are high, her mouth small and round and red with lipstick. So beautiful. Her gaze is sad.

"What is it you want?" she says. "My husband is sick."

"Treats," Kervin says. "For the performance. To celebrate the season."

"Rosquillas!" someone yells.

"Donkey's Milk," another shouts.

"At least some fruit," Kervin says. "Everyone has fruit to spare."

The woman frowns. "I have nothing," she says. Her knees bend. She slides down the doorframe a centimeter at a time. Slow motion disaster. "There's nothing."

The boy clings to her sleeve, afraid and lost. Inside my heart, it's like a river damming with silt.

Silence replaces hymn. Thoughts of a virgin's purity give way to the impurities of life.

This time, I start, walking onto the porch, opening my sackcloth, dumping it out. Oranges and sweet rolls, candy, a candle. Everything onto the porch by the door.

Kervin and the others follow, a steady procession of gifts poured out, a growing heap of treats. The boy's grip relaxes. The woman's red lips form *Gracias*.

And then I am flying to the next porch, Kervin hot on my heels. Soon there will be fireworks.

Reveal

Sacred in This Light

Sirens call like cats. Heat shoves at you, tightening the skin of your cheeks and forehead until you feel encased in shell. You watch orange fingers stroke roomfuls of furnishings, dance along a skeleton frame. People gather, eyes fixed on the flowering inferno that was a three—story home.

Beautiful, you want to say. The way the flames cooperate to crisp and consume profane shrines made by human hands, the sparks like flocks of angels overseeing demolition. Form into energy, structure into heat. You want to state these truths for the cosmic record. Of course, you do not. They would take it wrong, these people. They live in this neighborhood. In their eyes, the blaze could be their own house burning. And it could be, but that's not the point.

Wood smoke penetrates your lungs. You exhale, feeling an echo of liberation. The soul is smoke, life a parade of pretentious ambition and catastrophic event. In the end we are all destroyed. You don't say this either. There may have been people in that house, dogs and cats, certainly cockroaches. No, you dare not voice such philosophies tonight.

A beam gives way, screaming a glorious shower of white—orange embers. A forge of creation before your eyes. You ache to speak. What point is witnessing if the witnessing is not shared?

"It's ..." You stop. The crowd has stepped back, leaving you alone on the sidewalk. Do they think you fearless? Will they hear your praise as poetry, or something else? "Never mind," you mumble, looking down. The top of your head warms and dries.

The ground is a battlefield of shadow and light. Do worms worship flame? Will ants build monuments to this night? You

85

look around. Glittering eyes, downturned mouths, everywhere masks of dread and sorrow. Is there no one who understands, no one who feels the glory of this blaze as you do?

A uniformed man pushes at your shoulder. "Back, sir, back." A helmet encases his skull. You watch fingerlike reflections squeeze and recede. You hold your ground.

"Please, sir. This area is not safe." An ember settles on his shoulder. You watch it flare, skim over, recede to dull orange glow. A life lived in seconds, the journey exposed in fast motion. Emotion swells through your chest. The blaze has revealed itself upon his shoulder.

A baton between his hands compels you back. You feel panic, a sputtering sense of drowning. This is your last chance to say something, anything, to mark the event.

"I did it," comes from your mouth. "I started the fire." It's like a bubble releasing, a bright spark from the darkness inside you. You feel relieved.

The policeman transforms, a different kind of heat colors his wooden face. As he reaches, you sense perhaps this is one more thing you should not have said.

The Lecturer

The lecturer is rather dishy, with a mop of black hair and the bluest eyes. He wears a white lab coat over black jeans and a tee shirt with writing across the chest. I can only read a few letters through the gap:

NTS TO

EEP

TH M

ANTS TO KEEP BOTH MEN? I wonder. Just where would the ants be holding these men?

The lecturer strolls the aisle, passing out a packet, standard pencil, and tick sheet to each participant, all the while going on about his research background, which seems to consist of focus group experiments in pop culture. *The impact of Madonna's wardrobe on male saliva generation, How football color impacts in−game violence, as measured by ...*

ENTS TO WEEP WITH ME? I do admire a man that's sensitive to ecology. My last lover, James, planted a container garden on the flat's roof. I used to lie awake after we made love, thinking of roots growing down through the shingles and tarpaper, winding through the ceiling. Would I wake up cocooned? Maybe our bedroom would be made into a museum. See the root mummies? See how they cling to each other even these hundreds of years later? Oh, how they must've loved. Oh, the passion they must've felt. Sometimes I wish it would've happened like that. At least I'd be giving something to the future. I wouldn't be barren old Wanda, nattering Wanda, Wanda who drove her fiancé away before the first tomato bloom.

The lecturer gives me the packet and sheet. I smell a hint of soap. He even washes his hands. It's hard for me to meet a man's eyes directly, but I force it now. There's gentleness in that blue. That's how Geoff's eyes were. Geoff came before James. Which goes to remind me that the eyes might be windows onto the soul, but might not be the best indicators of a long–term relationship. Much like stiletto heels might shape a model's calf, but leave me limping to the Metro.

He starts back toward the front of the room. I should've sat closer than the last row.

"Today," he says, "we shall examine an unusual trait in humans, where some people taste a particular chemical, while others don't taste it at all. Why these different responses? What's the survival advantage? Data we collect today could help to figure that out."

He leans over a projector. I glimpse a bit more of his slogan.

E

ANTS TO

LEEP

TH M

REMOVE PANTS TO SLEEP WITH ME? I know that must not be right, but it brings a blush to my face. I reach down and undo the top button on my jeans. That starts up a pleasant tingle.

"... phenylthiocarbamide," he's saying, "or PTC. The TAS2R38 gene encodes a taste receptor on the tongue that affects whether someone can taste PTC."

I watch his mouth move, his lips, his tongue. I wonder what it's like to shag with this lecturer. Is his tongue glib in bed, or is he one of those grunters who think their pumping weight is enough?

88

"Differences in genetic make—up are genotypes," he says. "The ability to taste is a phenotype, an observable effect of genotype."

Is the ability to fuck a genotype? I wonder which gene I have. James and I never talked about our sex life. I don't actually know how he perceived me as a lover. Did the mere thought of me make him hard, or did he have to work just to make a go? Why do we never discuss these things? Why spend time on politics or BBC programming while our basic needs go unmet? What I need is a lecturer who brings my clitoris to attention, right?

The projector projects a Neanderthal man. I raise my hand.

The lecturer looks up. "Yes?"

"I was wondering if you keep office hours."

"I do," he says. "Talk to me after the experiment."

"Oh, fine," I say. "I'm sure I'll have a million questions."

He returns to his presentation. I barely watch, thinking of his abs pressed to the curve of my spine, his kneecaps to mine. A yin— yang in the making.

The projector clicks off. Overhead lights come on.

"Questions?" he says, looking directly at me. I shrug down in my seat. *Later*, I think.

"Okay, then, let's proceed with the experiment." He directs us to open the packets. There's a paper strip inside.

"I want you to suck on it," he says. "Don't worry, it's sterile."

I follow his command without hesitation, imagining his finger pressed between my lips.

"What do you taste?" he says.

Taste? Nothing. My mouth is empty of sensation, entirely lacking.

"There's a box for sweet," he says, "and sour, bitter, or none. Please tick the one that best approximates your reaction."

I pick up the pencil. I press it to the *None* box, but do not mark. What will he think of a woman who cannot taste?

Up and down the aisle, pencils scritch. He comes around to collect the items, mine last of all.

"Can I see your shirt?" I ask him.

He frowns, then smiles. "Sure." He parts the lab coat to reveal:

HE

WANTS TO

SLEEP

WITH ME

My spirits sag like a Birthday balloon gone flat. The way he presses his hands to his hips confirms it. *Gay.*

I sigh, and move my pencil to the Bitter box. A quick 'X' and I am done.

Meringue

Jeremy was embarrassed his mother made him take Home Ec. But she was such an imposing woman. Her love was like a vice squeezing him.

And so, here he found himself standing at his workstation, surrounded by pimple–faced girls and girls with big butts and girls with long hair bound up into buns and tucked under plastic caps, and him alone, longing for release from … well, everything.

He watched Jelsey's lithe brown fingers open an egg shell, watched her pour the yolk back and forth, tendrils of clear liquid draping between the halves. He watched her hands, her wrists, the backs of her arms, the way her shoulders kneaded, the nape of her neck, the tip of one ear.

In his copper bowl, yolk swirled through whites laced with shell. His fingers did not move like Jelsey's, his hands could not caress, his shoulders were blocky things. And his head was … well, in another place.

Jelsey dumped yolk into a measuring cup. Jeremy swiped egg shells into the trash.

"Now," Mrs. Tegolfski said, "take the whisk into your right hand." She tittered. "Unless you're left handed, of course."

Jeremy frowned. Mrs. Tegolfski was fragile and passive, the opposite of his mother. He didn't want to do anything she said.

"Hold it firmly, like so."

Jeremy reached down. He watched Jelsey pick up the whisk and position it above her bowl.

"Now we will beat the whites," Mrs. Tegolfski said. "Ready?"

"Ready," the class repeated.

"Insert the tip gently. Begin to whisk, but not too hard. It's in the wrist, students. Watch my wrist. See? Small strokes, quiet, barely lifting. Only a little movement, no splash, no noise. The mucous will begin to liquefy. The globules shoot up, and everything collapses into foam. You should feel a thickening."

Jeremy mimicked Jelsey's motions. He watched the jiggling of her flesh, her arm, her breast. It was working! He did feel it, his fingers curled around the shaft, a relentless thickening.

"Now," Mrs. Tegolfski said, "gradually, increase the breadth of your strokes, and their speed. Continue to beat with these larger strokes, faster, harder. See how the foam smoothes? It should be white now, bright as a bed sheet. Now, take the whisk out and turn it over. The foam should form a tassel like the one on your graduation mortar should you pass my class." She tittered.

Panting, Jeremy leaned onto his arms. Jelsey's face was flushed too.

One by one, Mrs. Tegolflski inspected work stations. "Excellent Allie. Great job Graylinda. That's wonderful Jelsey." She came to Jeremy, and stopped. Her mouth formed an "O". Her eyes widened, irises vibrating as they took in the slimy mess at Jeremy's workstation.

"I think there's been a miscommunication," she said at last. "A terrible miscommunication."

Jeremy wiped his hands on his pants, the whisk untouched on the counter. He wondered if maybe his mother had wanted a girl.

Cat

Cat was feral when I found her. It took a dozen cans of Dinty Moore to gain her trust. A year for her to crawl onto my lap. Now she hunches deep inside the cage, eyes smoldering.

I reach. She does not lean into my cupped palm, or even acknowledge my attempt.

"It's only for a day." Once my voice might have drawn her from her instinct. I pull back. One by one, my fingers lose contact. I withdraw my arm. She does not look away.

"One day," I say softly.

"Animal!" she hisses as I climb the basement steps.

His Father's Nose

A car accident left Tyler badly scarred. He hadn't been properly buckled into his child seat. While the air bags deployed to save his mother's face, his own impacted the driver's headrest to devastating effect. A broken jaw, three teeth ripped out by their roots, a cracked orbital socket and torn lip. Against all odds, his nose came through unscathed.

"A minor miracle," a doctor told a nurse.

"He's just adorable," the nurse replied. Only a woman would say that, looking at the shattered terrain of Tyler's face.

Sixty—eight stitches and two surgeries later, he was mostly recognizable as the rascal he had once been. Those gleaming blue eyes had not changed, nor had his high energy diminished. Still, there was something different. He became wary of the world around him, wary about adults, fussing when they held him, ducking away from head—pats.

"You can't blame him," Grandma said.

"I don't," his mother answered. "I just wish he would let me hold him once in a while. He's all I have."

Grandma nodded. "He has his father's nose."

Tyler couldn't leave that alone, so he asked about his father. There was some sort of mystery surrounding his father's death. Grandma distracted him with toys, as she always did, but his mother broke out crying.

That night she came to Tyler's room, and showed him a photograph. Dad's gaunt face stared into the camera, scabbed cheeks and neck, a frantic want in those blue eyes to either side of a proud, prominent nose.

"Drugs, baby," she said. "Cocaine. They couldn't bring him back."

She tried to hug Tyler. He curled down inside his blankets and pretended to sleep. Now, he knew his dad. He could see those eyes whenever he wanted. He'd just look in a mirror and remember the crash.

When Tyler started first grade, his teacher's name was Miss Moody. It fit her perfectly. One day she would yell at Tyler to pick up his crayons, the next she would beg the other children to please not torment him. Tyler took it all in stride. It wasn't such a big deal to jam a few wax sticks into a box, and the other kids didn't really bother him. They were just curious, maybe a little jealous. He didn't mind the attention.

One day a man came to their class. He wore a suit and tie, and the lenses of his glasses were thick.

"Okay, children," Miss Moody said in her listen—to—the—teacher voice. "Gather around for story time. Mr. Mark brought a book to read to us."

Grudgingly, Tyler followed the flow of kids to the classroom center where chairs had been arranged. He found himself staring at Mr. Mark's glasses, the way they magnified his watery eyes. He wondered what his own face might look like through lenses. Would scars become rivers? Would screwed—in teeth stand out?

"Tyler," Miss Moody said. From the tone of it, it wasn't the first time.

Tyler drew his focus. "Yes, Miss Moody?"

"Mr. Mark asked you a question."

95

"What do you want to be?" Mr. Mark said. His huge eyelashes blinked. "What do you want to be when you grow up, Tyler?"

Tyler laughed. "That's easy. I want to be like my dad."

Mr. Mark nodded. His lips revealed a line of white teeth, though his eyes wanted to look away from Tyler's face.

"And what does your dad do?"

"He died from taking drugs," Tyler said.

Now Mr. Mark did turn away. Miss Moody looked disconsolate.

"He breathed it," Tyler said. He'd done some research since his mother told him. "Up here." He touched his perfect nose, and grinned.

Lactose Intolerant

Jimmy always fell for the cool girls. There was nothing logical about the urge, just an electric want skittering along the wires of his spine. A girl in sunglasses sent him mooning; a girl with a gun gave him the sweats. The ultimate addiction? A girl in sunglasses with a gun, who showed no interest – zero, zilch – in his pathetic self.

Jimmy saw her in WalMart. It was a busy Saturday and there she was, wheeling a plastic shopping cart topped with shrink-wrapped steaks and sausage links through the masses of grazing shoppers. She wore a camouflage tee shirt – desert, not jungle – and crisp brown slacks. A handgun was holstered on the efficient half-curve of one hip. Wrap-around shades hid her eyes.

The cart possessed a serious wobble, a catching front wheel that seemed determined to alter her course. She pushed relentlessly through its tantrums, leaving little skid marks on the linoleum. There wasn't a hint of frustration on those slanting cheeks, that thin-lipped mouth. Jimmy found it all fascinating.

He tossed a pizza box into his own cart, and set off in pursuit. It pushed his limits to catch up to her, but he did.

"You've got a bad wheel," he said. It was the Dairy Aisle, the air cool against his skin, a hint of curdle in its scent.

She turned. Jimmy saw the shadows of unblinking eyes behind her sunglasses. He felt suddenly exposed, which only heightened the sense of dangerous thrill.

He gazed at the sidearm, and his hackles went wild, buzzing and yearning in the same instant. *Flee!* his hormones screamed. *Stay,* he told himself. He wanted to touch her holster.

97

"Is it loaded?"

She gave him a hint of a smile. "Think you can take it?"

Jimmy nodded.

"Knock yourself out." She shaped her arms like a gunfighter, hands open but away from her hips.

Screw it, Jimmy thought. He closed his eyes and lunged. His body hit hers. He imagined a linebacker diving into a running back, the football squeezed between them. A resounding crash sounded. Tubs of butter spilled from the shelves. A bag of shredded cheese exploded.

He grabbed her wrist. The gun has half–drawn in her hand. Grunting, he tried to pry her fingers loose.

"No," she panted, leveraging her other arm against his chest. With a massive shove, she rolled him along the dairy case, and yanked the gun free. Now he leaned across the case, face up. She stood over him, gun sighted on his forehead. All around them, people stared.

Jimmy smiled. "You're pretty strong." She nodded, cheeks ever so slightly flushed. The gun barrel did not move.

"Help me up," Jimmy said. The electricity of the moment had given way to a dull sense of accomplishment. This was one impressive pick up line.

Her lips parted, exposing teeth.

"Help me," he said, extending his hand. His hip throbbed. "You win. I'll buy you dinner, how's that?"

"No." She thumbed the safety off.

"Seriously?" Jimmy said. "Dude. I learned my lesson. You put me in my place."

"Not yet," she said, and pulled the trigger.

The Bestseller

There was a suppleness to Ellen that made her stand out in the crowd of hard women she ran with. One sensed she might wear a bra like I did, and that it might bear at least a hint of lace. Whereas the others were intent on erasing gender, Ellen spoke of equal pay or equal treatment with a subtle tilt of face that told me it was only rote, not heartfelt rhetoric. I was pleased when she was chosen to represent them.

I was to sit on the management side of the table, the other side of the moon that demarcates enlightenment from delusion. Some called my promotion sheer tokenism, but I had earned it. I'd slaved on that floor for years, kept my nose clean, my foot pressed to the pedal through break time and lunch. Why did these girls think they deserved more? What sort of entitlement mentality had set into these piecework women?

After the negotiation, after their pathetic union caved, there was gossip that Ellen and I had become lovers, as if I were some common butch trawling through a heap of pieceworkers to sate her lustful thirst. We were not – and I cannot emphasize the point more forcefully – we were *not* lovers.

I did, however, fantasize. I watched Ellen through the observation window as she inspected a blouse or fingered a buttonhole, and those full lips would suddenly press onto mine, those long fingers would glide down my neck, my bosom, my ribs. I found my fingers mimicking hers down to my skirt, and in, and down, and in again, and I … well, let us say that events took their course in my office.

Afterward, I retired to the bathroom down the hall. It wasn't much, but did have a stall. As I sat there, heart fluttering like an ill-strung harp, it came to me how silly I had been to risk my career on something as foolish as fulfilling base desire on company grounds. For a time, I simply sat, and then I peed. As I stood, I glimpsed a face floating on the polluted water in the bowl, Ellen's sweet, elastic cheeks, the eyes wide open. It was imagination, of course, and yet she was very real in that moment.

I flushed, let the basin fill, and pulled the chain again. Thus were my guilt and remorse expunged, and her image in my mind put back into its place. I suppose you could call it catharsis.

It was then that the idea came to me for the book, though it took many years to reach publication. The rest, of course, is history. So, yes, there *is* a kernel of truth within the story. I altered her surname, and the key event was only imagined in real life. Dramatic license they call it, or maybe wishful thought. But I do hold out to you that even one experience can change the arrow's flight of a life. Do you not agree? Well, you are very young.

To whom should I make the inscription? Honestly? Ellen? How delightful. It must be true that names come around in cycles. There, how's that? You remind me a little of her, actually. Perhaps you would like to discuss the book further over lunch?

Coffee

He looks out over the city and thinks of death. Somewhere down there in the pit of this valley someone's dying, curled into a ball in that dead end alley next to Ralph's Surplus maybe, or leaning lopsided with a Lucky Strike smoldering between veed fingers.

"Donut?" the counter clerk asks.

He pulls his gaze from the window. She's pretty in a homely way, with curling brown locks that look entirely unmanageable, and a determinedly defiant jaw. Her skin is caramel brown.

"A dozen?" she says. Her eyes are bright somehow, like the lull in a storm when you can see lightning so clearly without having to endure its lash.

"Coffee," he says.

"What kind?"

He squints at a menu that makes no sense. "Black?"

"Half," she says without batting an eye. "My dad's white."

An intense embarrassment overcomes him. His tongue twists for words.

"I'm just joshing with you," she says. "You want sugar in that coffee?"

He nods mutely. She turns, and drains coffee from a stainless steel urn into a Styrofoam cup. He watches her move, the way her hand goes to the swell of her hip. She's been on her feet too long. Her hip aches, there in the hollow beneath the ribs.

He can't help but think of the pain his wife endured in those final months after they gave up on chemo. He can't help but recall the pain his son expressed this morning. Another argument, another slugfest, only this time he'd landed a punch, a real one.

"One lump or two?" It's the clerk.

"No," he says, the shortest answer. She fits a lid to the cup, slides his coffee across the counter.

"A dollar–fifty–nine," she says.

He digs through his pocket for change. Three quarters, a dime, six pennies. It's not enough. His thoughts go purple, a throb like the swell on his son's pudgy cheek. *Death*, he thinks. Death of flesh, death of love, death of dignity. He's stared into the black eye of a gun a couple times, but hasn't been able to make that coward finger squeeze.

"I can't …" Rope constricts in the pit of his belly, fibrous strands poke from a smooth weave. Coins clatter on the counter. The clerk slides them onto her palm.

She opens the register, deposits them. "It's okay," she says in a voice gone quiet. "The shit isn't worth what they charge." Her teeth are not straight, but they remind him of his wife's.

She touches his hand. "Rough day?"

He looks at her fingers, the knuckles weathered, fingernails chewed to stubs. She has her own problems. Still, he can't help it. He nods. He meets her gaze. For just an instant it's like staring into the barrel of that gun, only it's light inside, not dark. He thinks of the time he helped his wife plant a walnut sapling where the elm came down, their gloved hands touching.

103

And then the moment is gone. "Thanks," he says. He takes the cup, feeling its warmth, thinking how muted it must be compared to the boiling liquid inside.

Life he thinks, turning from the counter. The clerk swivels her attention to the next person in line.

Plymouth

Kemekitchi trotted through the white oak forest carrying his bow in one hand. The deer's blood was falling faster now, two strides apart instead of three. His arrow had penetrated the animal's shoulder and sent it running. It would not last long.

A sweat lodge vision had shown him that this buck would stagger into their village and infect his people if they ate of it or wore its fur. Recently, Micmac warriors had encroached on Wampanoag territory and the Sachem had sent many warriors to fight them. The evil spirit, Hanegoategeh, was taking advantage of their absence to deliver disease through the stag.

Forest gave way to straggly pine. More blood and a clutch of fur marked a berry bush along the fringe.

Kemetichi paused. Less than an arrow's flight ahead, the ground ended at a rocky beach overlooking the sea. That was where the blood was leading. Excitement warmed him. He thought of his friends who would be spared by his quick action. He thought of the eagle feather he might earn.

The buck lay dead upon its side, eyes glazed. Blood leeched into the sandy soil, which supported tufts of grasses and bunches of lavender flowers. A boulder leaned over foaming waves like a clam diver preparing to jump. Worry replaced Kemekitchi's anticipation.

"What am I to do?" he whispered. The animal was dead, but the demon certainly was not. It could have seeped into another living thing, perhaps the grass or the flowers. He would have to burn the

105

carcass and every bit of vegetation within reach. At least it had chosen a poor place to die, thank the Great Spirit, for the soil was too thin to support tree roots. He would not need to destroy the forest.

For three days, Kemekitchi worked. He burned the buck. He dug up flowers and pulled grass, and tossed that onto the fire as well. Great billows of smoke flew into the sky, obscuring the sun as thoroughly as a pigeon migration.

Only when his work was finished, did he eat and drink. Muscles aching, he moved away from the leaning rock. He would remain for a day. If a sprout should erupt, he would destroy it. Hanegoategeh could be most persistent, it was said.

He awoke to water splashing his face. Reaching for his knife, he sprang to his feet.

Three pale men stood before him. They wore stiff hats, bent up on one side and pinned with a golden eagle. One pointed a musket at his chest. Kemekitchi spread his hands, and dropped the knife. He had witnessed musket fire as a boy hunting with his father. It was not fear he felt, but calm acceptance. He had no quarrel with the pale men.

The one with the musket pushed him toward the charred area. Another knelt and prodded the buck's bones, while the third inspected the leaning rock.

"English?" the musket man said.

Kemekitchi shook his head. The musket man shrugged. The man by the rock began picking at a patch of lichen.

The spirit! "No," Kemekitchi said. He lunged, pushing the man away from the rock. "It is not safe. We must leave this place."

Too late. The lichen was on the man's fingers. The musket barrel struck Kemekitchi to his knees.

Kemekitchi tried to stand. The lichen man pushed him down. Where he was touched, Kemekitchi felt spores digging into his skin, seeping into his spirit. Already, he sensed a dark disease inhabiting him.

The musket man barked an order. The others pulled Kemekitchi to his feet. Now his heart did beat fast with fear. He imagined spores spreading to the third man, to others on their giant canoe, to Wampanoag villages along the coast; his friends and his mother and his sister dead, everywhere death.

Kemekitchi's courage fell like an eagle losing its draft. A searing pain pushed up his throat. Sobbing, he cupped his face into his hands. The evil spirit had won.

Deep beneath the stony earth, he heard Hanegoategeh laughing.

Years of Feast and Famine

February 17, 2007 began the Year of the Pig according to the Lunar New Year calendar. It was on that date that I started my quest to become Earth's fattest man. A side of bacon for breakfast, three Big Macs and triple fries for early lunch, then a plate of ribs at Zibo's an hour after that. Dinner was the immobile meal. I would routinely stuff myself so full of potatoes and pasta, with occasional salad (heavily dressed, of course) that I could not move from the sofa for hours. I began relieving myself into buckets. My wife complained, but kept cooking. I loved her more than life itself, but not more than a good steak rubbed with pepper and cooked over a low, blue flame.

February 7, 2008 brought in the Year of the Rat. I was at 390 pounds, and growing fast. I had been given permission to telecommute, and routinely did my job as a traffic analyst while chomping down bags of Doritos, Cheetos, and pork rinds. Coke was my morning drink. At noon I switched to sweetened tea, with so much sugar you could watch it precipitate out when you put the pitcher in the fridge. This was the year I began my affair with Meghan Chives. Almost every night after my wife was sleeping, blindfolded and tooth–guarded in her bed, I would squeeze through the doorway and make the laborious trek three row houses down to Meghan's. We would eat greasy chicken or meat skewered on metal. I think it was the adrenalin fear of discovery that drove me that year, though it could also have been that Meghan's cupboards were well stocked.

2009 initiated the Year of the Ox. I was over 500 pounds now, and every movement became a labor. I was dragging the world around. No surprise when the company laid me off. Times were tough, and my work had degraded. It's difficult to click when your finger is larger than the mouse button. I stopped my affair with Meghan. Lugging my heart monitor and O2 tank was not worth the reward.

2010, the Year of the Tiger. I took charge of my weight gain with a vengeance. My wife, with Meghan's encouragement, it turns out, had been working toward staging an intervention. They even arranged for a famous weight clinic to hoist me out of the apartment and put me under house arrest. There were whispers of stomach staples and liposuction. I put a stop to it. I was not about to waste three years.

2011 was the Year of the Rabbit. And it's true that I now had to forage for myself, nibbling through our pantry one shelf at a time. A difficult year, best left unrecalled. My wife was gone, and so was Meghan. I lost nearly a hundred pounds.

2012, the Year of the Dragon. I have refocused on weight gain, even as it consumes my hoard. I will soon be forced to return to my women for nurture, and I will do so without regret. It may take a week to make it down into the basement where the freezer is, but I will make it one way or another. And they will be there.

Next year begins the Year of the Snake.

The Story of Johnny Zig–Zag

Johnny, he be down here long as most. He a second generation zig–zag child. Now, don't you go looking like that at Johnny, not no girl like you, born to the high end. He ain't gonna work no miracles on your particular want. You come down here all like a martyr and that, you not be one of us. Not yet.

Hand on over that cigarette. There you go. That be one step closer to all right. Ah, I feel that silksmoke down deep in my crinkled lungs, like that first day of spring when the snows done gone and the river be running too high to sleep under the bridge. You understand, girl? You ever sleep under no bridge? Didn't think so. Here's your fag back. We share down here in the mercy mile, don't care what no one says, we share what we got, even if it be nothing much at all.

Here be the thing about Johnny. He start out smaller than small. Him Ma be a single ma, oh 'bout twenty years back. You should of seen this old city then, girl. That tower over yonder? There be a clock up there then, and it strike the hour clear as the bell in your baby blue head. Things used to be different down here, and they just maybe will be again.

Anyway, Johnny's Ma, she be down here selling her time when that clock strike one particular day, and out of a cab steps Johnny's Dad in a brand new suit. They say it were the first look that sold her. He was yo–oung, sixteen, and his first time downtown too, and his smile be like staring at the sun. I expect that why Johnny got you looking too, and his voice, I guess. And those muscles. He sweep floors at the Y, and they be letting him use the weights. Keep him Johnny if you know what I mean.

So, there be his Dad standing on that curb, and his Ma gaping something fierce, and they sort of run into each other accidental

110

on purpose. Well, she go down onto the cement, arms and legs widespread, and he fall right on top. There be some discussion to this day how it happen, but when they get up, Johnny's Ma be pregnant. Didn't take her long to show it neither. And then Johnny come bouncing into the world, perfect as can be, and his Ma decide she be keeping him.

Like any mama, she go after Johnny's Dad for support. Now, he be only sixteen, remember, and live with his ownsome parents, who got no good use for a woman like Johnny's Ma, and not even that much for a son that knock one up. I see you know what that mean. When you expecting, child?

Well, Johnny's Dad, he be throwed out his parents' home, no money, not much educating, just that fancy suit to sell for food. Which he do, right quick. They take up with zaggers over on Fifth and Pine for a time, but the pickings be lean, so they come down to the river and hole up in yon drain pipe. It got grated and padlocked after the riots. You want more about that, go on down to the library and ask Jan. She real good about helping us, and everybody else.

So, there they be, a thirty-some woman and her boy husband, and a baby on their hands. Soup kitchen help them for a year or so, then they be begging their way into a room above the Diamond before it burn to Hell. After that point, it be back to the zig-zag, back to the mercy mile.

Johnny's Ma, she die the next winter. Some say food poison, some say STD. Johnny's Dad, he don't last much longer. Drive by took him down. They say he bleed enough for two, and his last word be, "fuckers", which maybe show where Johnny come by his tongue.

He growed up fast after that. Oh, he had me and a few of us to watch out for him, but he not be needing much of that. He born for the zig, I tell you, bred to the zag. Before you knowed it, he

111

be the top of the crop down here, and he don't owe no one nothing for it. Make him stubborn confident. Johnny do what he want, and he know what he want, too.

They say he feed you if you hungry, heal you if you sick, make you warm if you be cold. He lift you up out of black despair, and bring the light back. But first, you got to be one of his flock, you got to get his desire.

Me? I be down here nigh on fifty years, girl, got more dead in me than alive. But you got a stretch ahead of you. Walk the mile, learn the zag. When you dirty enough, when you not still thinking like no rich girl, you catch Johnny's eye, I know it.

Him Ma, she weren't no virgin, but him Dad, he probably were. If one's good enough for the likes of Jesus, who to say it ain't good enough down here?

Distort

Glass Animals

As best Malcolm could read, the sign said "No Glass Animals in Pool". The sign lied. Standing on the diving board he saw them: glass crocodiles, translucent hippos, sharks. They skimmed just beneath the surface, yawned cavernous mouths through passing wave troughs. The skin of his shoulders bunched.

"Come on," Janiqua said. "Don't be such a chicken." She fidgeted on the diving board to his right. Her board dipped and rose, making a rhythmic squeak.

"I ain't chicken," Malcolm said.

"Whatever." Squeezing her nose between her fingers, Janiqua leapt. The board chattered. Malcolm watched her woman hips lift and twist, watched her hand come down off her face and lead her to the water. At the moment of impact, Malcolm saw shards, a bright welling of angles and planes. He imagined his brother's forearm, a needle digging like a shovel lifting grass. Malcolm smoked weed, but had resisted the hard stuff his brother sold. Even so, his future looked grim. This last suspension was about to turn into expulsion. The advocate had told him to brace himself. Without school, there was no way out of the hood.

Water splashed his baggy swimming trunks. Janiqua was in the pool, glass animals snapping after her. He watched her panicked strokes, her thrashing legs as she tried to escape them. If he was smart, he would jump now while they were distracted.

He bent his knees, and let his weight sink. The board bounced, but he pulled back from the actual leap. Him escaping anything was about as likely as jumping and not coming down. Gravity was another rule on another sign he could not read.

117

At the far end, Janiqua pulled herself over the pool's lip. Teeth clung to her, fell away as she stood, drained back into the pool. Malcolm looked down. Glass animals were already jostling for position beneath him, mouths and eyes snapping.

"Come on, Malcom!" Janiqua wrung the ropy wads of her hair. "If I can do it, you can. Ain't nothing you can't do if you set your mind to it."

What the hell, Malcolm thought. *Maybe gravity is wrong too.* Maybe he would jump and never come down, just lift up and up, above the pool, above Janiqua, above the rusted chain link fence, the battered water tower, the boarded crack houses on Sampson Street, the whole damned city, up and up and up until he would never have to come down again.

The muscles of his legs gathered, his breath sealed in, his heart calmed to a steady pound. The board bowed beneath him, closer to the pool. Glass animals pushed up from the water, strained to reach his feet, chlorine breath hot on his skin. But he knew the board would rebound. It would bear him up, and throw him high as the other board had done with Janiqua. If he had faith in anything it was consequence.

And then he was rising faster, lifting up. As his toes lost contact, he felt the sky open.

118

The Thing About Domination

It was a tall tree, taller than our three-story house. I looked up and up, bare branches, angular divides, twigs stretching like fingers into the space beyond the tree's grasp. It wanted more. It wanted everything, all the air, the sky itself.

The roots were just as bad, clawing between the rocks permeating our lot, doing battle with worms, heaving sidewalk squares up. *Who needs frakking when we have this tree?* I thought.

"Up you go," my wife said. She was squat and dumpy, with coal black eyes and prominent brows. A smile would break her face.

"I don't even see him now," I said.

"It's up there," she said.

"Maybe he went in the squirrel house." God knows I would have, were I a squirrel.

"It did no such thing," she said. She raised an arm. I flinched even though I was out of reach. "There," she said. I saw him then, a spray of brown fur tucked into a niche between branches.

"Maybe he has a nest," I said.

"What it has," my wife said, "is a squirrel house. And it will use that house, or I'll know the reason why."

"Yes, dear." I let my shoulders slump. The tree would not appreciate me scrabbling up its bark.

"I didn't say tomorrow," my wife said. I felt her moving close.

"Right." I launched myself up. Bark scraped my wrists. My fingers became claws. I grasped a branch, another, and pulled myself higher.

"Hurry," my wife said. "Before it moves."

Blood slicked my hand. I lost my grip and I was falling. The feeling that came into me was unusual, not fear, not longing, but some hybrid of the two. Branches caught me. I found myself sitting on a clump of interwoven twigs.

"Well?" my wife said.

I edged back to the trunk. The squirrel house was only a few feet higher. A week earlier I had screwed it to the trunk with black multipurpose screws. I'd borrowed a ladder from a neighbor then. Why hadn't I thought to do that now? I glanced down at my wife impatiently tapping her foot on the crooked sidewalk. Question answered.

A foothold, a handhold, and I was at the squirrel house. From a higher branch, the squirrel started chattering. His tiny hand pointed at the hole in the house's side.

I peered in. The interior was furnished with a table and two chairs. One looked to be a recliner like the one I preferred in our house.

"I –" I looked again. A lamp stood between the chairs, spilling golden light. I wondered where he had found a bulb to fit it.

More chattering. The squirrel gestured emphatically.

"Inside?"

He nodded, teeth showing. They were rectangular, and quite yellow.

"I can't fit through there."

"Grab that rodent and force it inside," my wife demanded. "Do I have to come up there?"

"No, dear," I said over my shoulder. "I'll try," I whispered to the squirrel.

It was easier than I thought, a matter of pulling myself over the hole's lip and sliding in.

"What are you doing!" my wife screamed. "Get out of there!" Her voice reached a higher register, like the wicked witch in Oz.

The table held blueprints. I sat in the recliner. It fit my body perfectly. Something clapped the outer wall.

"She's throwing my walnuts back at me," a new voice said. It was gentle, like water easing over stone. *The tree?*

The squirrel came in. A chatter came from his mouth.

"He says you took long enough," the tree translated.

"I didn't know it was possible," I said.

"All things are possible when you stand up for yourself," the tree said. Another slap hit. I heard my wife talking to herself.

"We're glad you came here," the tree said. "She'll have to find another weapon now."

"Weapon?"

"Shall we discuss strategy?" the tree said. The squirrel nodded. His tail flicked.

"I'm afraid I don't understand."

"We're going after her garden," the tree said. "An outflanking maneuver. We have allies among the birds and insects." The squirrel made a fist.

121

I chuckled. "You don't know my wife."

"We know that she means to dominate," the tree said.

"And you don't?"

"We are of Nature. It is our destiny to dominate."

"You poor fools," I said. Even as the words left my mouth, there came a subtle shaking, followed by the hacking sound of an axe applied to wood.

"Hey," I said brightly. "At least you tried."

A Consequence of Copulation

Churly turned. "The maggots in Love's eye will not copulate."

Basco's lips curled down. "What of Hate?"

"The same," Churly said. "Maggots propagate in the meat, but not in the eye."

"This is problematic," Basco said. He pulled levers. Lightning raged between the poles of his Tesla coil. "I do not wish to corrupt the meat of Love and Hate, merely their mechanism of sight. Their subsequent blind thrashings will destroy polite society, and I shall be held blameless."

"Perhaps … ?" Churly said. His face was bulbous, and tinged green from certain other experiments.

"Yes, yes," Basco said. "Out with it."

"Perhaps, if they themselves copulate?"

"They themselves?" Frown dented Basco's high forehead.

"If they, you know, do it, perhaps the maggots will get the idea."

Basco pushed levers. The laboratory shook with thunder. "Ludicrous!" he screamed. "Lascivious!" He returned the levers to their set point. "Try it."

And thus were Love and Hate brought to the padded room and encouraged to *relate*.

"So," said Love, twirling her hair. "Do you come here often?"

Hate rose up before her, his prodigious member pulsing. "Not really," he said in a voice that recalled Basco's thunder. "You?"

123

Now Love stood too, breasts heaving. "My first time," she said. A white worm pushed from her eye socket. A black worm exited Hate's heart.

Sometime later, Basco yelled, "Is it working? Is the experiment a success?"

Churly pulled his face from the peephole. "I cannot tell," he said. "The room is full of flies."

The Patron

A sign said *Join the Zoo*. A girl in a red smock tended the booth, looking as dispirited as I felt after nearly two years unemployed, and six months without a home.

"What's in it for me?" I said. The world had taught me some hard lessons, one of them being that no one does anything without expecting something in return.

She appraised my dust–caked beard, and glanced at a clipboard in her hand. "How about an electric razor? A nice, clean shave."

I could tell by her lack of emotion that she needed me. Never show desire, lest it be used against you. This girl had a quota to fill, and I was the only ambulatory man in sight. Men are not joiners. This zoo must have a shortage of males.

"Don't need a razor," I said.

She frowned. "Do you own one?"

"You'd be surprised what people throw out." I produced a comb from my pocket, and proceeded to brush my hair. Many of the teeth were missing, but my hair had thinned anyway.

The girl looked again at her clipboard. "You can choose a meal," she said. "Dinner at Bob Evans. You could order fried chicken and potatoes, with apple pie and milk."

"How long?" I said.

"How long?"

"How long do I have to join for?"

125

"Oh," the girl said. "One year. I can sign you up for more, if you want. It's a better deal."

I snorted. "It would take a hell of a lot of fried chicken and pie for that." I rubbed my belly, trying not to look hungry.

"For two years, you get a phone," the girl said.

The tip of my tongue swiped cracked lips. It was tempting. "No thanks," I said. "My freedom is worth more." The phone was probably solar powered anyway, useless in the long night.

The girl looked confused. I was breaking through her defenses.

"I'll join your zoo on one condition," I said. "Let me touch you, hold you in my arms, lay down beside you overnight. A day and a night, that's my price."

"I don't think you understand," she said.

"I do. I know how the world works. It begins with a promise, a pretty girl, a deal too good to pass up. It ends with me locked inside a cage, naked, on display for children. 'See the ugly man? See what becomes of you when ...' And they'll point to the sign: *Homeless Erectus*. And they'll laugh, and nudge their spouse and wink at the cleverness of it."

The girl's lips turned down, her eyes focused on mine.

"I'll do it," I said, trying not to watch her transformation. "Where do I sign? What do I do?" In truth, it was a welcome relief, the promise of being done with this existence.

The girl set her clipboard aside. She touched my face.

126

Bullet

There's a bullet with your name on it, scratched letter by letter with a penknife. A memento of my love. That final "A" was the day I lost my foot to an IED. Then you dumped me. I threw that slug as far as I could. After our Skype this morning, I'm looking for it again. Sam dumped *you*? You're *willing* to take me back? You have no idea how that makes me feel. So, yeah, I guess you could say I'm still interested.

Madonna

Blood is her gift, her curse, flooding the marbled architecture of her veins, coagulating from her sacred loins. Life—nurture, life—sacrifice, duality, the price of her pedestal.

Nora's RV

Nora had always been the responsible one in their household – hers and Joe's – but her sense of duty took on a new dimension this Tuesday morning, an inflated desire to nurture and protect and upkeep. She rubbed her face and got out of bed. She made breakfast for Joe, and bundled him off to work. She fed tuna to the cats, Sine and Cosine (Joe's idea, not hers), then unwound the vacuum cord for a quick go at the area rug in the living room. In the kitchen she heard the parakeets chuttering, and imagined Sine sitting below the cage, tail twitching. He knew better than to jump, didn't he?

She switched the vacuum on. A sense of empowerment thrummed through her. God's voice, not words, not even thoughts, but the rumble of something really, really big. She barely noticed the debris being swept up into her device. She put the vacuum away.

Her period was a couple days late, so she did a pregnancy test, peeing on the stick, waiting impatiently for results. She spied mold on a section of tile grout above the tub's rim. *Scrub it later.* She tapped her foot. Her watch ticked off the final seconds.

Negative. She didn't know what to think or feel. She and Joe weren't married yet, and he wasn't pushing for a family, but she was broaching 30. How long should they wait?

She ran cold water at the pedestal sink. There was that voice again, vibrating deep down in her brainstem. She wanted so badly to understand it. She knelt onto her knees and prayed as she had not since childhood. *Get it right, Nora.* How many times had her father said that? How many times had she heard it? The answers were not necessarily the same.

129

She finished, stood, stretched. In the mirror her eyes were bluer than she recalled, or maybe she'd never looked before. Her stomach was flat. Negative. Wasn't that how miracles worked?

She thought of the vibrator tucked into her nightstand. It reminded her of the vacuum, of the faucet, of Joe. She went to the bedroom and stripped off her clothes. She lay on the bed, and opened the drawer. Fingers trembling, she reached inside.

Later, it was God's name she cried out, God's pillow she clung to. But Joe's musky smell. Maybe that was a sign. Maybe that was what the voice had said, that she needed to awaken to the signs around her.

She heard a plane fly low. This happened occasionally when the wind shifted from its prevailing direction, and the airport adjusted. The windowpane rattled. In a flash it came to her. The world was about to end. What else could this morning mean? She rinsed the vibrator and put it away, then scrubbed the grout and ate lunch.

Afterward, she rounded up Sine and Cosine and packed them into the pet carrier. There wasn't much room, but enough for them to curl around each other. She thought of babies curled into her womb.

The parakeets were next. She took the cage from its hanger and set it beside the carrier. Sine rumbled low in his throat. Birds fluttered to the opposite side of their cage. Nora nodded. They would have to learn to coexist. No one said saving the world would be easy.

When Joe came home from work, Nora was washing the RV they had bought used the summer before. The plan had been to take a month off and travel, but the plan never materialized. Too many bills, too many obligations Nora could not release. Joe never complained. This ought to make him happy.

"Hi, Hon," he said, pecking her cheek. His blue mechanic's shirt was stained with oil and sweat.

"Get changed," she said. "We're taking a road trip."

"Today?"

"Why not?"

"I have to work tomorrow."

"Call off."

"Where do you want to go? Did you see an ad on the TV?"

Nora dropped the sponge into the bucket. She wiped her brow. Joe's eyes fell to her wet t—shirt. That always made him hot.

A dog loped down the driveway, a clumsy Dalmatian with lolling tongue. The neighbor's dog off his leash. Again. Nora opened the RV door, and enticed him inside with a handful of cat treats. He slobbered on her hand, tail wagging. She closed the door, and stepped down.

"You want me to take him home?" Joe said.

"No," Nora said. The dog yapped, and scratched at the door. "We're taking him with us."

"What?" Now Joe looked more concerned than confused.

"I'll explain while I drive. Go get changed."

It took more cajoling, but he finally put on a tee shirt and clean jeans. He came outside, sipping from a beer can and looking more relaxed.

"Where are the cats?" he said.

"In there." Nora nodded at the vehicle. By now the dog had settled. The parakeets called out every once in a while, but the RV was mostly quiet.

"What gives?" Joe said. "You're never impulsive. This is more like something I would suggest. What happened?"

"The world's ending," she said. She walked around to the driver's side, and got in. She inserted the key into the ignition. The engine coughed and started.

The dog came forward, panting. Would Joe join them? He would if he felt it as she did, that vibration deep down in the Earth's mantle. She had until midnight. It would be a full moon tonight. She'd looked it up on Google.

She put the RV into gear. The passenger door opened. Joe climbed onto the seat.

"I don't know what's going on here," he said, "but I'm not going to let you go off on your own."

"Good," she said, pressing the gas pedal. The vehicle lurched. The dog stuttered forward and back.

"What about dinner?" Joe said.

"We'll eat on the road."

They stopped at a McDonald's near the Interstate. Joe ordered his usual meal. Nora got a salad.

A mangy mutt scrounged around the dumpsters out back. Its white fur was stained nearly black, and one eye looked infected.

"Get it," she told Joe. "Use your burger."

"What?"

"We need another dog." She explained to him they were saving the world. She needed pairs of animals. Singles were no good.

"That's … crazy, Nora."

She gazed into his eyes.

"What if it's another male?" he said.

"Get the dog." She slipped her fingers into his. "Please?"

"This is ridiculous," he said, opening his door. A few minutes later the two dogs were sniffing and growling in the back, parakeet feathers settling all around.

They bought leashes at WalMart. Nora took the Eastbound entrance to the Interstate.

"Where are we going?" Joe said. The sun was beginning to set now, creating a reddish glow in the rearview.

"Mount Ararat," Nora said. "It's about five hours."

Nora found an ant crawling on the dashboard, and urged it into her empty soda cup. A few miles later, she pulled into a rest stop. While Joe walked the dogs, she found another ant. It was larger and had different coloration, but it was the one she found. The first ant was curled around a droplet of soda in the bottom of the cup. It was not dead. She trapped two flies in Joe's cup, and pressed the lid on tight. The persistent buzzing they made reminded her of her inspiration, devotion, whatever it was.

They stopped for gas. Nora stood outside, the pump humming beside her.

"We need mice," she said. Insects, mice, cats, dogs. An ecosystem.

She had Joe empty the toolbox in the back of the RV, and sent him into the tall grass of the lot beside the gas station.

He returned empty–handed.

"It's not your fault," she said. "It was the wrong place. It's not like I have an instruction book."

Joe shook his head. He smiled, then laughed. "I did find something." He cracked open the toolbox enough to peek inside. Two crickets skittered. He closed the lid, and took it into the RV.

Nora resumed her place in the driver's seat. For a moment, she let herself listen to the steady thumping of the crickets' efforts to escape, tiny heartbeats competing for attention. *If you knew what was coming, you would not want to escape*, she thought. She pressed her left hand to her stomach. She turned the key in the RV's ignition with her right. The engine came to life.

"Did you hear a voice?" Joe said.

"I just know," Nora said. "I prayed." She reached across, and patted his thigh. He took her fingers into his hand.

Outside, the sky blackened. Nora yawned. She was getting tired, but dared not stop. Joe turned on the radio. It was mostly static.

"Did I ever tell you about the book I read in college?" he said. "About the bicameral … bicaramel … some sort of mind?"

"No."

"Well, it was by some researcher who claimed that our brains have evolved since the Greeks. He said the gods used to speak to us, a part of our brain that's been lost or changed or something."

"Interesting," Nora said.

"He said it was like hearing a voice in your head, the right side, I think. No wonder they had so many gods."

Nora smiled appreciatively, and listened to Joe explain in more detail. She could not help but think God had put that book into his hands ten years ago to prepare him for this night. Without the book, would he have accepted her claim? *Mysterious ways*, she thought, and shifted lanes to pass a beat up station wagon.

"Mice," she remembered. She pulled off the interstate. They found a pet store, and bought two white mice. On a whim, though she understood there really were no whims on this night, she purchased a male and female hamster as well.

"Fish?" Joe said. He'd always wanted an aquarium. *Why not?* Nora thought. She had kept the credit card paid down. Joe bought two neons, two swordtails, and a couple of black mollies. When they hit the road, a ten gallon aquarium graced the floor between front seats.

"Do you think it's enough?" he said. Nora glanced at the dashboard clock. 10:55.

"It will have to be," she said. She scanned the black horizon.

"What are you looking for?"

"High ground," she said, recalling the story of Noah. "We're not going to make Ararat." She had no idea how God meant to end the world, but as Dr. Phil had drummed into her, *the best predictor of future behavior is past behavior.*

"Knob Hill's off Exit 135," Joe said.

"Does it have another name? Something Indian maybe?"

"I imagine so," Joe said.

135

Nora took the exit. The road became bumpy, the animals became restless. Nora began to have second thoughts. What if she was wrong? What if she had dragged Joe away from his work for no reason? She'd charged up the credit card, for God's sake.

"No doubts," Joe said. "It's the same with my work. Sometimes I'll get a feeling what's wrong and I just have to trust it and hope I got it right." He laughed. "You know what?"

"What?"

"I almost always do."

"Thanks, Joe."

"For what?"

"For believing."

They started up an incline. Headlights burned twin slivers of clarity through the dark. Soon, the road was switching back upon itself, and back again. Nora felt the altitude more than she could gauge it with her eyes.

"It's not the highest mountain," Joe said, "but it's the highest around here."

"It will have to do," Nora said. They hit a bump. Water splashed. She heard a fish flapping. Joe bent down to retrieve it.

"There's a flashlight in the glove compartment," Nora said.

"Of course there is," Joe said. "And you wonder why I trust you." The incline steepened. The RV strained to keep up momentum. "Come on, darlin'. I should have tuned the engine."

"There wasn't time," Nora said.

"How long do we have?"

"Fifteen minutes," Nora said.

"That's not very long."

"No, it's not."

The road began to level. Nora pulled into a parking area overlooking the valley. Lights littered the blackness below in patterns too large to interpret. She shut the engine off.

"We're here, I guess," she said. She pulled a blanket from beneath her seat, and stepped onto asphalt. A burp rose from her stomach. She swallowed it back.

"What about the animals?" Joe said.

"They'll be fine."

"Are you sure?"

"No," Nora said, "but I believe."

She spread the blanket beside the parking lot. They sat together, looking out over a sea of lights. The vibrations were muted now, damped by miles of stone between them and it, whatever *it* was.

Joe slipped his arm around her. "I'm glad I came."

"Me too," Nora said, leaning into him.

They watched the world below.

Sons and Fathers

This is the book of the killing of Jesus Christ, the son of David, the son of Abraham.

Isaac killed Abraham; and Jacob killed Isaac; and Judas and his brethren killed Jacob; And Phares and Zara of Thamar killed Judas; and Esrom killed Phares; and Aram killed Esrom; And Aminadab killed Aram; and Naasson killed Aminadab; and Salmon killed Naasson; And Booz of Rachab killed Salmon; and Obed of Ruth killed Booz; and Jesse killed Obed; And David the king killed Jesse; and Solomon of her that had been the wife of Urias killed David the king; And Roboam killed Solomon; and Abia killed Roboam; and Asa killed Abia; And Josaphat killed Asa; and Joram killed Josaphat; and Ozias killed Joram; And Joatham killed Ozias; and Achaz killed Joatham; and Ezekias killed Achaz; And Manasses killed Ezekias; and Amon killed Manasses; and Josias killed Amon; And Jechonias and his brethren killed Josias. And after they were brought to Babylon, Salathiel killed Jechonias; and Zorobabel killed Salathiel; And Abiud killed Zorobabel; and Eliakim killed Abiud; and Azor killed Eliakim; And Sadoc killed Azor; and Achim killed Sadoc; and Eliud killed Achim; And Eleazar killed Eliud; and Matthan killed Eleazar; and Jacob killed Matthan; And Joseph the husband of Mary, of whom was born Jesus, who is called Christ, killed Jacob.

And we said unto God, "Why hast thou created a world of such murderous nature, O Father?" And He said unto us, "You have eaten of the fruit of the tree that was in the midst of my garden. Thus shall it ever be, my children, that the son murders his father by inches, and the father gives life to his son. The husk must crack so that the seed may flourish."

Gold Standard

Shelly injected gold leaf into her veins. Her thinking was that as it settled out she would become both more valuable and less vulnerable. Instead, she nearly died from blood poisoning. Her skin turned the color of tarnished copper. Her insurance refused to pay for chelation therapy. Her boyfriend dumped her. Her boss fired her. She returned home to a stack of unpaid bills and a dead cat. In due course she was evicted. Now she roams the streets, turning tricks to get by. "All because I tried to make something of myself," she explains in her more lucid moments.

Cheshire Cheese

Their host, Arthur Hatter, was said to be something of an oddball. Alice was nonetheless pleased to be invited to the Forty—Second—and—a—Half Annual Cheese Tasting and Debauchery Party at the Cheshire Mansion. It indicated a rise in her local stature. In a village comprised of writers it was nice to know her work was being read and appreciated.

The invitation had come in the form of a tiny book with blank pages, but for the final one, which proclaimed, "The End!" in a flourished calligraphy not unappealing to Alice's gaze. She wondered if Hatter had done it himself, or hired the work out. Might she expect to receive a contract from him should she catch his wandering eye?

The carriage pulled through a circular drive cobbled in horseshoes that made the wheels rattle and the horse team quite uncomfortable. They skittered sideways and back, seeking footing atop those upended feet.

The carriage rolled to a stop before ornate double—doors featuring twin knockers the size and shape of breasts. On each, a brass ring dangled from the nipple. Alice blushed. Only this morning, Jack had touched her bosom for the first time, a glancing stroke. His face turned from the carriage window. He nodded at the empty place on the bench seat beside him.

"No," Alice said. "This is neither the time, nor the place for passion. You may, however, kiss me." She leaned forward. No kiss forthcame. Instead, Jack huddled in the corner, looking dissolute.

"Were I to kiss you now," he said, "it would be as a house built over a volcano spout. It might begin innocently enough, but the lava ... oh, the lava!"

"What?" Alice said. Jack often made no sense to her. She produced the invitation from her hand–purse. "Will Lord Hatter mind that I brought a guest? The invitation did not specify."

Jack took the book, and produced a magnifying lens from his inner vest. The book held open between the fingers of his right hand, he stared intently through the glass in his left, his eye now larger to Alice than his not insubstantial nose.

"'Arrive together, come alone.'," he read. "I wonder what that means?" He turned the tiny page. His brow furrowed. "'It means bring a guest, you idiot, but expect debauchery of the lowest order.'" The book fell onto his lap. "It answered my question."

"Nonsense," Alice said. "You're making that up." She retrieved the book, and dropped it into her hand–purse.

"You're the writer," Jack said. "If anyone made it up, you did."

Epiphany rinsed through Alice. *Perhaps I did, at that.* She glimpsed an image of her fingers poised above a toothwork of capital letters, a bar that said "Space". She pressed it with her thumb. "Space," it said. "Space, space, space, space ..." She felt herself falling.

"Alice?" Jack held her. Her face pressed his neck. She smelled musk. Warmth swirled up from her groin, fighting the cold downward draft of logical thought. Books that answered questions, driveways cobbled from horseshoes, machine visions. Something was very ... off.

"A momentary dizziness," she said. "We should go inside."

"If you say." Jack stood. Alice's mouth formed a circle. Jack's codpiece was suddenly huge, a bulging orange dome about to erupt. She tried to blink, but something stopped her. *Of course.* She sagged with relief, and pulled the magnifying lens from her eye. Jack's codpiece returned to normal.

"I believe this is yours," she said, handing the device over. Jack looked vaguely disappointed as he pushed through the carriage door, and held it for Alice. She stepped onto the runner, then solid ground. *Too solid.* The walkway was formed of stones shaped like the soles of boots and shoes. She now stood on stones that exactly matched her feet.

At the door, Jack took an inordinate time to work the knocker. His fingers caressed, his palms cupped. He lifted the ring with delicate precision, licked his lips. Alice stood stiffly all this time, the most curious feeling inhabiting her. When the knock finally sounded she felt its reverberation deep down in the private places of her soul. This was where darkness lived, where wildness prowled. She prayed Jack would not notice.

The door opened onto a man wearing a ludicrous top hat. "Alice!" he exclaimed. "Jack!" He did a jig, hat wobbling. "Alice and Jack, Jack and Alice. Welcome. Do come in."

A servant took their wraps. Another offered wine in glasses shaped vaguely like hourglasses. Where one bugled in, the next bulged out. It was like a puzzle on a platter. Alice sipped. She nearly choked. The wine was salty. Was it wine at all?

"Mine own vintage," Hatter said. He led them down a wide corridor to a ballroom colored pink. Inside, a table stood.

"Have you no other guests?" Alice said. "Did we arrive early?"

"Read your book," Hatter said. He seemed distracted, leaning over a platter at the table's end. It held a casserole of some sort, the color vaguely orange.

142

Alice opened her invitation. The first page was blank again. She turned to the second. On it, a single word: "No." The facing page held an equally simple, "No."

"No no?" Alice said with a frown.

"No, I have no guests," Hatter said in an irritated tone. "No, you did not arrive early." He slapped his thigh. "Must I do it all for you, Alice?"

"It all?"

"Turn the page," Hatter said.

Alice did. The print was tinier here. She barely made it out. "'Your guest is as good as mine'?"

"Time to eat!" Hatter screamed.

There were no plates. The table was bare, but for the strange casserole, which Alice saw now was molded from various cheeses into the shape of a cat with an overlarge head.

"Cheshire cheese," Hatter said. "It's contagious."

Jack licked his lips. "Where do we begin?"

"With the tail, of course." Hatter doffed his hat. Inside, a serrated blade the length of his wrist. He deftly cut the tail free and gave it to Jack.

Jack ate quickly, smacking his lips between bites. "So light and airy," he said. "Such a tangy taste." Hatter carved the flank for himself, leaving the torso and head for Alice.

"I couldn't," she said. "With my fingers?"

"And your mouth," Hatter said. His teeth were coated orange.

Alice felt suddenly ravenous. She dug in with an appetite she never knew she possessed. The taste was salty like the wine, but somehow pleasing too. She ate and ate, her fingers griming with cheese, her tongue slick with it.

Then the feast was done. She felt as if she had eaten three wheels, an entire table of cheese. Yet the head remained.

It smiled. It winked. "Just when you think you've tasted everything," it said, "there's always something more."

Funny Stuff

Saturday nights, I hang out in the alley behind the Revco waiting on my buddy to empty the trash. He always stuffs a bottle of *Dopa—Meme* in the bag, and I pay him a little something for it at church next morning. Works like clockwork, only tonight I was a little late. I checked the dumpster, rifled every damned bag. No bottle. No happy pills to carry me through the crappy night, no belly laughs to lubricate my loneliness.

Now, I'm not one to howl at the moon when I'm hurting, but it was pretty bad. The shudders, the sobs, indigestion, you name it. I hadn't laughed in days, hadn't even smiled. I didn't know how long I could last, if you want to know the truth. A man without laughter is like music without sound.

I was heading back toward the street when a side door opened. Laughter spilled into the alley, a flood of the stuff, and out pops this guy in oversized pants and Bozo hair. The door closed. Laughter gone. I pulled my arms tight around myself, and I do mean tight. You show a hungry dog that steak bone, take it back, and see what it gets you.

"Hey," I said. "You the one making those people laugh?"

He turned, eyelids flapping.

"Did you make those people laugh?" I said.

Creases formed on his white—paint forehead, parallel chasms as dark as the alley. "I got my share. What's it to you?"

"What's it to me?" I pointed my finger like a gun. "I want laughs, you got laughs. Hand 'em over. And no funny stuff, if you know what I mean."

145

"Huh?" His nose spun around. Water shot from a flower pinned to his chest. That was exactly what I was talking about. He's lucky I didn't blast him.

"And take off that goddamn nose," I said.

"Nothing, huh?" He detached the nose, and stuffed it into his overstuffed pocket. His real nose was fleshy–flat. He nodded at my hand. "What're you going to do with that?"

I pulled my thumb, and made a clicking sound with my tongue. The clown's shoulders slumped. "You're serious, then."

"Too serious," I said. "Way too fucking serious. I haven't had so much as a chuckle all week, I'm so serious."

"Okay," the clown said. He raised his hands defensively. "We can talk this out, right? Don't do anything you'll regret."

"The pills," I said. "I know you took them." How else could he have made that audience laugh? He was as funny as jock itch.

"What pills?" he said. His lips went straight, but his face continued to smile. Irritating, to say the least.

"The pills you found in that dumpster." I pointed back along the alley, and he took the opportunity to bolt.

I formed my left hand into a gun and fired overhead. "Bam!" the sound echoed. The clown stopped in mid–stride.

"I don't use pills," he said, turning slowly with hands raised. "You have to believe me."

"Prove it," I said.

"Ask anyone. Just open that door, and –"

"Make me laugh," I said. "You must know a joke or two, right?"

146

"I got a million of 'em," he said, and seemed to relax. "What do you call a cow with no legs?"

"Not funny," I said.

"I didn't do the punch line."

"Next."

He sighed. "Okay, okay. How about this? Two peanuts are walking down the street. One is assaulted." He rat—a—tatted his index fingers.

"Where are the pills?" I said. I pointed square at his face.

"Okay, okay," he said. "Look, I found them in the dumpster like you said, but they're gone now. I used them. I had to spend the whole bottle on that crowd."

"You're holding out," I said.

"No," he said. "No, really. It's the God's honest truth."

A shivering fit overtook me. I couldn't stand it anymore. All this unfunny drama in this humorless alley. It was too much.

"Sayonara," I said, and pulled the trigger. "Blam!"

For a long moment, he just stood there, face shifting through broad emotions: pain, anger, remorse. The creases in his forehead reappeared. He looked down at himself, his arms, his stomach. He felt his throat and ribs.

"You missed." His mouth mimicked the smile on his face.

"Did I?"

The flower on his chest quivered. Blood oozed from its center, and began to flow. The clown gasped. He clutched at the flower, and fell to his knees, then backward onto his back.

I walked to the corpse, and stared into those glassy eyes. I felt bad. I wouldn't have done this if he hadn't found the pills, if I wasn't late, if, if, if … No number of ifs will turn a wish into fact.

I searched through his pocket: squishy nose, entwined handkerchiefs, lipstick. Underneath the junk, I found what I was looking for. My hit, my dope, a single capsule of *Dopa–Meme*.

"So, you *were* holding out," I said. I popped the pill into my mouth. The taste was salty, then sweet. The churning in my stomach stopped, reversed direction.

A giggle bubbled up. "Look who's laughing now," I said. Before I knew it, I was laughing so hard I had to hold my sides. That over–painted clown bleeding in the alley was the funniest damned thing I ever saw.

Monkey On My Mirror

I had been driving south on Highway 75 for a few hours. It was a clear day and the traffic was light. Consequently, I was in that zone between alert and asleep, eyes fixed incoherently ahead, thoughts drifting to the hum of tires over asphalt, the regular heartbeat of seam joints and patched pavement.

The radio scanned from one fading talk station to the next. So many strident, argumentative voices. All I wanted, was peace. I had watched my sister buried that morning. The viewing yesterday, her face empty of emotion, hair carefully combed and laid across her shoulders as if she'd worn it that way in life.

Peace was what I needed now.

Ahead, a moving van clipped along at a steady 60 mph. I glanced at the outside mirror, preparing to pass. I did a double take.

A monkey with blond−red fur sat primly on the mirror housing. I gaped at him. He gazed at me.

I took my foot off the gas. The seatbelt harness resisted my momentum. The monkey was unaffected. I blinked and blinked again, but he remained in place.

"What are you doing?" I mouthed. He continued to gaze. I pressed the window button. The pane buzzed down. Wind shook my hair.

"Where did you come from?" I said. "How did you get there?"

The monkey's glistening eyes watched.

"I've been driving too long without a break. Is that it?"

The monkey scratched its side.

"What do you want?" I said.

"Can bald men get lice?" it said. I watched its mouth, designed for howling, form words as smoothly as any person.

"What?" I said.

"A bald man," the monkey said. "Can he get lice?"

"I ... I don't know. I'm not bald. I don't have lice."

"You know what bald is," the monkey said. "You know of lice."

"Well, yes," I said, "but I don't ... I mean, I've never thought about it."

The monkey nodded. "Look in the mirror."

My gaze went to the reflective surface. I saw a hand reaching, *Hope* stenciled on its palm. Startled, I swerved. The front tire hit a rumble strip, sounding a mournful whine. My bones and teeth stuttered.

There. I'm awake now. I guided the car onto the travel lane and resumed a normal speed. The moving van had pulled ahead.

The monkey was still there. I felt an urge to push it. I stopped myself. There was such tranquility in its posture, the slack expression, those gentle eyes. The peace I craved.

"Hope," the monkey said, "is memory reversed."

"I don't understand."

"And you say monkeys lack cognitive complexity."

Anger blew through me. I pushed the gas pedal. Now, the monkey did seem to notice. Its weight shifted. It looked annoyed.

"Man is the only creature that refuses to be what he is," the monkey told me through the window. I smelled meat on its breath along with something sweet.

I frowned. The only thing I refused to be today was grieving. My sister was the last family I had, but death happens, right? You can't change it. She had a couple kids out there somewhere, products of a long ago marriage, but I'd lost contact. Water under the bridge.

"You claim to look forward," the monkey said, "but you are only capable of looking back."

"Nonsense," I said. "You're a monkey." Now I really hit the gas. The monkey's arm shot out. It grabbed the slanting window frame. Such tiny, human fingers.

"You imitate," it screamed, "derivate, recapitulate."

"Recapitulate? I don't even know what that means."

The monkey laughed a high–pitched chatter. It reminded me of Meghan when she was young, playing in the neighbor's pool while I watched from our yard.

"Show me," the monkey said.

"Show you what?"

"Show me that you can apply knowledge forward."

"How do you mean?"

"You want to pass that truck, correct?"

"Yes."

"You mean to pull into the passing lane, correct?"

"Of course."

"Drive straight through it instead."

"That's ludicrous."

"Is it? Your Physics suggest that matter is only loosely packed. Passing this truck should be merely an issue of moving your mist through the mist of its existence."

"I don't know. I'm not a Physicist."

"I do," the monkey said. "And I'm just your basic primate."

The van was close now, only yards beyond my hood, my fingers, bloodless white, clenched so tightly I felt the steering wheel shape the meat of my hand. How had I become so wound? It must have happened gradually, like soil scraped from a grave so slowly you don't notice what's happening until a face appears, dead and cold, and you see it's your sister, the girl you hated and loved throughout your empty life. There it is, you can't look away, you can't go back. You can't go forward.

I remembered sitting on the porch swing with Meghan when Mother died. We'd started with tea and ended with vodka straight from the bottle. I hadn't felt so close to her since she stood with me against those bullies in high school. I remembered the jut of her chin, her trademarked tangled hair, cheeks red with emotion. Oh, how I loved her in that moment.

I pounded the steering wheel. I slammed the gas pedal. The car jumped. The monkey flailed. Its tail wrapped the mirror stem. Fur bristled from its tiny skull, shaped by the screaming wind.

"Ha!" I shouted. "I made you move."

Three yards, two, one … The monkey's mouth opened, revealing savage canine teeth. I saw the mirror, still visible through a gap between its arm and ribs.

In it was my sister's face.

152

Pathways

Pavement. Buildings. Windows like vast blinking eyes. For a moment he is lost in the unfamiliar labyrinth, adrift amid swirling echoes of stone and metal, a heaving pulse of people, like blood cells at microscopic scale. (I was a scientist). He turns in a circle, staring up through a slowly spinning gun sight of white stone smudged with black, into God's wide open face. (Do I believe in Heaven?)

"Tourist," someone says in passing.

"Have you seen my daughter?" he yells after them. She should be here. She should be walking with him through this city. (Does it have a name?)

Her hand grips his. Her fingers are small. (She's eight). "Remember when we walked in Denver?" she says.

"Of course." Denver was jagged skyscraper peaks on the verge of breaking through organic constraint to overrun the wrinkled suburban plane. In the distance, blue mountains capped white.

"Did you take your medicine?"

"Yes," he says. (I think so). A brain cratered black. (Is that me?)

"Houston?" she says. Her fingers are longer now. He feels her nails. (She's twelve)

"We walked the inner loop," he says. It was not easy without sidewalks. Houston was an aborted dream, plans gone awry under stress. Loop after loop it was supposed to be, but the cars came too soon, the buildings too fast.

"Remember the armadillo?" And she giggles in just the way he recalls her giggling as the armored creature scuttled from the bushes, trailing a fragrance of spoiled meat.

San Francisco was colors, the Painted Ladies and deep blue sea, roller coaster hills. They walked in morning. (All those steps!) He glimpses her in purple robes, a strange flat hat. (Mortarboard)

"Can we visit the Golden Gate, Daddy? I've always wanted." A part of him opens. His chest warms and flutters. Her eyes, so thirsty to see the world around her, a mind that would never fill up, never go empty. (Like mine?) A chill grips him. He tries to remember her name. (Carla. No, that was her mother)

Where is she? She should be here, walking with him through the city. (Does it have a name?)

Pittsburgh had hills, and winding, dipping blacktopped roads, and bricks and cement, even gravel. They never knew where they were in Pittsburgh, every step an adventure. (Like now?)

"Point Park is the confluence of the Monongahela, Allegheny, and Ohio River, Pap—pap." It's not his daughter's voice. Was there someone else? Passing faces give away nothing.

Damascus. Squat cookie—cutter buildings, limestone hotels lined block upon block. Laundry hung on balconies, a skirt—suited woman striding past careening cars, goats, horses, briefcase in hand. (And gold) So much gold. Shops brimming with gold watches and chains and necklaces, gilded smiles. Broken English. "Fifty American. Fifty, you understand?" His daughter was not in Damascus. He walked alone.

(She's not here either)

He whirls, straining to make sense of the sandstorm faces. She's not there. Buildings press down until he cannot breathe. Ahead, the street opens onto a broad avenue. There are no buildings on the opposite side, only trees and sky. He can breathe there. Mouth open, he dashes for the intersection.

Tires screech. A horn blares. Then he's scrabbling on his knees across grass. Trees envelope him. Shade blocks the sun. He wants to curl into a ball.

"Don't be a sillyhead," his daughter says. He glimpses her long legs, the white line on her knee from when the training wheels failed. He tries to call out. (Carla? Karen? William?) What comes out is a mash of syllables. He struggles to his feet, and continues.

The trees end abruptly. He hears water. Sidewalk surrounds a low structure formed of slanting black stone. (An obtuse angle is greater than ninety degrees.) He staggers over. It's a square. Water flows from four sides into a pit. A woman leans forward, finger touching stone. Names are engraved there.

He feels rescued. He searches for his daughter's name, or even his own. (Alexander Driscoll, PhD.) These names make no sense.

"Have you seen my daughter?" he asks the woman. "We're walking in the city."

The woman turns. She has a kind face. "What is her name? What is she wearing?"

He turns back to the water, the steady hiss, the gold dust glint of sunlight. Transfixed, he watches that laminar flow slip down, down, down into an insatiable depth.

The Science of Blooms

Ferns do not produce flowers, the experts will tell you. Ferns reproduce by spore, not seed, and have no use for blooms. But when you're there on that one dewy morning, when your vision clarifies and the thoughtlines to your brain run clean, you will see those tiny hands – row after row of green–veined palms – drawing your attention to a singular glow deep within.

Leaving the Garden

We dropped baguettes over Rouen, their golden crusts catching the sunlight as they fell. Through the scope I watched shrapnel crumbs fly out at impact, the rings of smiling faces around that point that formed a hungry bull's eye. I thought of the hundreds of people who would be fed, bone thin children, women with upside down mascara eyes, men grown saggy in the constancy of their defeat.

At Brest, we dropped oranges, crate after crate of citrus. I watched them fall in clumps through clouds gone gray, saw the spray of their impacts, one after another, a gleaming trail through the darkening streets. I heard laughter, the surprised laughter of children shooting squirt guns, women discovering love letters, men playing a sport.

In Gabes it was lettuce, spattering green explosions across that desert sand. I thought of shade and water, children swimming in silence while their adults looked on. Peace.

By Palermo we were hurling tomatoes. Red splashed the world below us, gutters filled with juice. I thought of the people who would be splattered, of seeds tearing their opened eyes. I thought of turning back, but I was not a pilot.

In Athens we dropped sausages, the casings bulged with chopped meat. I thought of the craters they would make, the haze of spices they would leave behind. I thought of old men and women clinging, children lying prone in the streets. I thought of my own death.

War became a blur of squashes and string beans, corn cobs, misshapen melons. I no longer watched through the scope, but stared blankly at the single vegetable in our payload, a swollen

157

cucumber suspended from the ceiling. That drew me back to myself. I thought of its torpedo shape, the denseness of its pulp. I wondered what would happen when it dropped.

Thanks

With thanks to

Nathaniel Tower and **Bartleby Snopes** for publishing *Into the Woods* and *Monkey On My Mirror*

Camille Gooderham Campbell and **Every Day Fiction** for publishing *Sky Blue Pink*, *The Butcher's Son* and *The Thing About Domination*

Meg Tuite and **Connotation Press: an online artifact** for publishing *Saint Peter's Penis*, *Sacred in This Light* and *His Father's Nose*

JP Reese and **Scissors and Spackle** for publishing *Last Call* and reprinting *Leaving the Garden*

Cheryl Anne Gardner and **Apocrypha and Abstractions** for publishing *Blemished*

Cynthia Reeser and **Prick of the Spindle** for publishing *A Formidable Joy*

Matt Potter and **Pure Slush** for publishing *You Say* Tu Dou, *I Say* Ma Ling Shu, *Christmas in Nicaragua*, *Meringue* and *Pathways*

Liz & Laura and **The Toucan Online** for publishing *The Girl Who Turned Down Pizza*

The editors of **Nib Magazine** for publishing *Collision Course*

Patrick Trotti and **The Short Fiction Collective** for publishing *Simply Salazar*

The editors of **Churches, Children and Daddies** for publishing *Jehovah Joint*

Dezarae Boyd–France and **Pipe Dream** for publishing *Would You Be Wiser?* and *Desperation*

Angelo Bergen and **Absinthe Revival** for publishing *Canis ex Machina*

The editors of **The Journal of Microliterature** for publishing *The Mailwoman*

The editors of **Spilling Ink Review** for publishing *The Lecturer*

The editors of **Foliate Oak** for publishing *Lactose Intolerant*

Mary Akers and **r.kv.r.y. Quarterly** for publishing *Coffee*

Douglas Macgowan and **6 Tales** for publishing *Plymouth*

Earl S. Wynn for publishing *Years of Feast and Famine* in **Linguistic Erosion** and *A Consequence of Copulation* in **Smashed Cat Magazine**

G.S. Evans and Alice Whittenburg of **Café Irreal** for publishing *Glass Animals*

Mike Joyce and **Literary Orphans** for publishing *Nora's RV*

Sarah Gerard and **Caper Literary Journal** for publishing *Sons and Fathers*

Sara Fitzpatrick Comito and **Orion Headless** for publishing *Gold Standard*

Paul Jessup and **coffinmouth** for publishing a version of *The Science of Blooms*

Randall Brown and **The Journal of Compressed Creative Arts** for publishing *Leaving the Garden*

Previously published

Canis ex Machina
Absinthe Revival
http://www.absintherevival.net/

Blemished
Apocrypha and Abstractions
http://apocryphaandabstractions.wordpress.com/

Into the Woods
Monkey on My Mirror
Bartleby Snopes
http://www.bartlebysnopes.com/

Glass Animals
Café Irreal
http://cafeirreal.alicewhittenburg.com/

Sons and Fathers
Caper Lit Journal
http://caperlitjournal.weebly.com/

Jehova Joint
Churches, Children and Daddies
http://scars.tv/ccd/

The Science of Blooms
Coffinmouth
http://coffinmouth.wordpress.com/

His Father's Nose
Sacred in This Light
St Peter's Penis
Connotation Press
http://connotationpress.com/

The Butcher's Son
Sky Blue Pink
The Thing about Domination
Every Day Fiction
http://www.everydayfiction.com/

Lactose Intolerant
Foliate Oak
http://www.foliateoak.uamont.edu/

Leaving the Garden
The Journal of Compressed Creative Fiction
http://matterpress.com/journal/

Years of Feast and Famine
Linguistic Erosion
http://www.linguisticerosion.com/

Nora's RV
Literary Orphans
http://www.literaryorphans.org/

The Mailwoman
Microliterature
http://www.microliterature.org/

Collision Course
Nib Magazine
http://www.nibmagazine.com/

Gold Standard
Orion Headless
http://orionheadless.com/

Desperation
Would You Be Wiser?
Pipe Dream
defunct

Formidable Joy
Prick of the Spindle
http://www.prickofthespindle.com/

Christmas in Nicaragua
Meringue
Pathways
You Say Tu Dou, *I Say* Ma Ling Shu
Pure Slush
http://pureslush.webs.com/

Coffee
r.kv.r.y. Journal
http://www.rkvryquarterly.com/

Last Call
Scissors and Spackle
http://www.scissorsandspackle.com/

Simply Salazar
(Short) Fiction Collective
http://shortfictioncollective.blogspot.com/

Plymouth
Six Tales
defunct

A Consequence of Copulation
Smashed Cat Magazine
http://www.smashedcat.com/

The Lecturer
Spilling Ink Review
http://spillinginkreview.com/

The Girl Who Turned Down Pizza
The Toucan Online
http://thetoucanonline.blogspot.com/